TEQUILA FOR TWO

An Althea Rose Novel

TRICIA O'MALLEY

Lovewrite Publishing

Copyright © 2015 by Tricia O'Malley
All Rights Reserved

Cover Design:
Alchemy Book Covers
Editor:
Elayne Morgan

All rights reserved. No part of this book may be reproduced in any form by any means without express permission of the author. This includes reprints, excerpts, photocopying, recording, or any future means of reproducing text.

If you would like to do any of the above, please seek permission first by contacting the author at: info@triciaomalley.com

*"The moon comes up and the sun goes down.
We'll find a little spot on the edge of town."*
— *Florida Georgia Line*

Chapter One

"WHAT'S UP WITH THAT?" I asked, straining my eyes at the line of people approaching our shop.

"Pagan festival this weekend." Luna shrugged her delicate shoulders, tucking a strand of her wispy blonde hair behind her ear. Clad in a white linen dress and with the highest cheekbones I had ever seen, Luna was all elegance and grace. If I were casting for a white witch in a play, she would fit the part perfectly.

In more ways than looks.

Me, on the other hand? Well, I'm more curvy than Luna with the grace of an elephant, I suppose. This past month I'd darkened the hot pink streaks in my curls to more of a deep lavender color, and white clothes and I do not mix – mainly because I don't corner well and have a habit of spilling things on myself.

"Friends of yours?" I asked, knowing that as a white witch – yes, a real one – Luna had some roots in Paganism.

"Not that I'm aware of," Luna hummed, raising a delicate eyebrow.

"How did we not know there was a Pagan festival this weekend?"

Luna shrugged. "It was in the weekly paper."

"You know I've sworn off the paper after Craig wrote up that article about you," I said. A month ago Luna had been falsely accused of murder, and even though we'd threatened the local reporter with some pretty inventive curses, he'd still written a fairly accusatory article about Luna. A small retraction printed in the paper after Luna was cleared of all charges had done little to change my opinion of him.

"We still need to think up a curse for him," Luna reminded me.

"I've got Miss Elva on it," I said, referring to our resident voodoo priestess. I trusted her implicitly to find the best revenge for this particular situation.

"That should do it," Luna agreed, pasting a smile on her face, as the line of people grew closer to our shop.

My name's Althea Rose and I, together with Luna, run the Luna Rose Potions & Tarot Shop.

She's the witch; I'm the psychic.

I can't help it – being a psychic runs in the blood. My mother is far more prolific than I, flitting from country to country to cater to the famous people she deems worthy of her readings. Oh, she's a diva, that's for sure. Most people would probably say I have a fair share of her attitude, but I like to think that I take after my easygoing musician father, who has happily followed my mother on her travels.

Luna snorted. "Easygoing, my ass," she murmured, her polite smile never faltering.

"Stop reading my mind," I grumbled, moving from the

white-and-gold upscale beach-cottage elegance of her side of the shop to the velvety purple den of iniquity on my side.

Okay, so maybe "den of iniquity" is taking it a little far. But my tarot card shop was exactly what you would presume one to be – there was even a leopard-print chair tucked away in a corner.

And a skeleton wearing a Ramones shirt was sitting on it.

Pulling out my phone, I reluctantly googled the local paper to find out more about this Pagan festival. Tequila Key wasn't exactly known to be a hot spot for festivals. Or for anything, for that matter.

We are a sleepy little Key, just a speed bump for tourists on their way to Key West. Most people simply pulled to the side of the road to snap a picture by the "Tequila Makes it Better" sign that some genius had erected by the marker off the highway before continuing on down to a livelier Key. Any sort of festival was bound to be the talk of the town.

"The New Crusaders, a revolutionized order of the Pagan druids," I read out loud, raising an eyebrow at my screen. "Sounds like radicals."

"Some may call us that," said a voice to my left, and I jumped. I hadn't realized that someone had slipped past my privacy screen to wait politely at the entrance to my shop.

At least six feet tall and rail thin, a man who reminded me of Gandalf stood at my door. His hair and beard flowed in long gray waves over his forest green ritual cloak, and his feet were encased in butter-smooth leather boots.

That explained why I hadn't heard his entrance.

"Hello," I said, unaccountably wary.

"Hello. I wanted to see if I could arrange readings for some of my group this weekend."

"I'd have to check my schedule," I said, pointedly not reaching for my schedule. Something about this man's vibe was making me reluctant to help him.

"I'll wait," he said with a smile.

"What's your name?"

"I am Horace, the founding member, and the organizer of this weekend's festival," Horace said.

"And what is this festival for, exactly?"

"Why, to celebrate the earth, the sky, the ocean…all the natural beauty of this place. And this weekend is the full moon which also coincides with the equinox. We'll be celebrating the Mabon festival, to prepare us for the darker time of the year," Horace said, sweeping his hand around in a grand gesture.

I swear his eyes seemed to light up when he talked about the "darker time of the year." And what was he doing wearing a ritual cloak outside of an actual ritual? Even I knew that's frowned upon.

"In Tequila Key? Granted, we've got a stunning coastline, but we are a fairly cluttered little town, if you hadn't noticed."

"You've some lovely natural spaces outside of town for us to set up in. There's a private campground that we've rented out. You're welcome to come. In fact, I insist," Horace said gravely.

"I'll get back to you on that one, Horace. I'm sorry, but I have a telephone appointment at eleven. I'll be sure to let you know about my availability this weekend. Cheers," I said, smiling brightly and reached for my phone.

Horace held my gaze for a moment, his eyes so light a grey that they were almost white, before nodding once and padding silently from my room in his leather booties.

And leaving me with an unsettled feeling as I picked up my phone to call my client.

Chapter Two

"THAT WAS A LITTLE INTENSE," Luna observed later that afternoon as the last of her clientele wandered from the shop, their hands full of goods. I'd just finished my last appointment and had stepped into her side of the shop to size up the damage.

"Sales look to be good," I said, noting that Luna's crystal tables had been picked over, as well as her handmade soaps and elixirs. Her normally impeccable shelves were disturbed, and I swear I saw a muscle in her cheek twitch as she assessed the disarray in her coolly elegant shop.

"Yes, quite good," Luna murmured as she moved to a shelf, pulling forward bottles of frankincense oil and straightening them so that their pretty white and gold labels faced forward. Sighing, I walked over to the worn barn-beam farm table with crystals scattered across the top. Knowing Luna, we'd never get out of here and to our after-work cocktail until order was restored to her displays.

"You'll need to restock your crystals," I said as I tried

my best to rearrange some of the larger pieces of quartz that were left on the table. Luna waved a hand from across the room.

"I've a new shipment in tomorrow. I'll be fine."

"So what do you think of this, um, Pagan festival?" I asked, tucking my hair behind my ear and doing my best to smooth my face into as nonjudgmental an expression as possible. Luna snorted, an unladylike sound coming from her delicate features.

"I know you don't particularly like Pagans but I'm kind of interested in going," Luna said.

"It's not that I don't like Pagans," I began, moving to straighten her hand-packaged soaps. "It's that I don't like groups that profess themselves to be radicals. At all. Radicals and fanaticism often go hand-in-hand. Which usually ends up badly, for everyone involved. That goes for any religion, not just Paganism," I said.

Luna shrugged and turned to me with a smile. "We're still going, right?"

"Oh yeah, we're going."

"You aren't just saying that to try and skip out on your magick lesson tonight, are you? It's a full moon this weekend, and you promised we would work on your circle casting."

So here's the thing. I'm a psychic. I read tarot cards, get glimpses of the future, can see spirits, read minds, and sometimes – it seems I can do magick.

Just over a month ago, when Luna had been accused of murder, I'd found myself in a sticky situation involving handcuffs and a hot man.

Not *that* kind of sticky situation.

My best friend Trace and I had been kidnapped when we had stumbled too close to discovering who was framing Luna for murder. Seems Luna'd had a premonition of danger, and she had insisted I learn a magick spell – and lo and behold – it had worked to free us.

Now Luna was intrigued. Convinced I had some magickal abilities – she'd been after me ever since to work on some spells with her. I'd avoided it for the most part as I'd been too busy bemoaning the fact that the current manslice in my life wasn't back in town yet, but I couldn't put off the manifestation magickal thingy she wanted me to do tonight any longer. After all, it would be another month before the next full moon and lord knows I didn't want to listen to Luna poking at me about it for that long.

"Of course. Can't wait," I said, lying through my teeth.

Luna snorted again and pointed a manicured finger at me from across the room. "You'll love it. Magick can be almost intoxicating, you know."

I raised an eyebrow at her. Like I needed anything else that could intoxicate me. Between R-rated dreams about my somewhat boyfriend, Cash, and my love of a perfect margarita, I figured I was good on the more intoxicating aspects of my life.

"You never know when it will help you," Luna pointed out and I had to agree that she was right on that point.

"You'd think I'm already more well-stocked than the normal person," I said. Which was true, after all.

"You are. But it seems that in a crisis you have a tendency to forget to actually *use* the gifts the goddess has bestowed upon you."

Hmpf.

"What are you trying to say?" I said, placing my hands on my hips and wondering whether I'd be able to get out of the magick ceremony tonight if I picked a fight with her.

"I'm saying that you are a stunningly beautiful woman whose own brilliance exceeds her sometimes," Luna said smoothly.

I squinted my eyes at her. Had I just been insulted?

"Flattery will get you everywhere," I finally said, accepting that I couldn't argue my way out of tonight's magick lesson.

And, let's be honest here: Me in crisis mode is akin to a fish being tossed out of the water onto the dock, flapping around desperately to try and figure out a way to save itself. It probably wouldn't hurt for me to have a few more tricks up my sleeve.

I sniffed again. Maybe there was something to this magick thing after all.

Chapter Three

"WHAT DO YOU mean I can't have a cocktail?" My voice rose as I eyed Luna across the living room of my house.

"You can't do magick when you've had alcohol. Something will go wrong," Luna said, giving me her *I'm serious* look.

"Whatever, *Mom*," I mumbled as I walked to the back verandah to throw the ball for the one constant man in my life, Hank, my Boston terrier. I smiled as I stepped out onto my covered porch, where huge palm-frond fans stirred the humid air, making it slightly less oppressive, and low-slung couches clustered around a few tables. Hank raced up from my slip of a beach, shaking the water from his coat and spitting out a stick at my feet.

"Take a dip, did you?" I asked, leaning down and tugging the stick from his mouth. Yes, he'd just dropped it at my feet, but as soon as I'd shown an interest in picking the stick up, Hank had grabbed it back, forcing me into a game of tug.

We're still working on "drop it," okay?

Finally winning the stick from him, I launched it into my yard and smiled as he raced after it, his sturdy little body wiggling in joy, his snorts of ecstasy echoing across the yard.

My house was the last in a row of houses in the old part of Tequila Key. The recently renamed Port Atticus was the new section of Tequila Key and boasted gated subdivisions and tiny spots of grass that were watered constantly. Pearls and golf shirts reigned there. I was much more comfortable with my side of Tequila Key, where the creatives and wanderers ended up, creating a mixed bag of cultures and skill sets.

My house was smushed up against a row of others; a semi-detached in realtor-speak. I'd lucked out – mine was the end house, nearest to the water. From the front, it just looked like a funky house, painted in bright colors with weathered plantation shutters framing the tall front windows. An outcropping of rocks and palm trees shielded the fact that my back yard – open to one side – had a tiny scrap of a beach that was all mine.

I'd put money down on the spot when I'd seen this house. One thing about the Keys is that if you can find beachfront property you can afford – buy it. It's much better than being stuck on the channels and having to motor out to the blue water that everyone actually wants to be on.

The inside of my condo boasted my sense of style, which was something akin to flea market meets photographer's studio. I'd renovated the house immediately upon buying it, knocking out the walls that had made it a true row house and creating an open first floor. I'd painted the walls a soothing grey and promptly covered them with miles of my underwater photography, in both black-and-white and color, and shoved all sorts of couches and ottomans throughout the room. It was eclectic, welcoming, and just a bit crazy. Kind of like me.

Well, I'm not entirely sure about that welcoming bit.

"He's having fun," Luna said, coming to stand by me as we watched Hank zoom around the yard in a fit of the crazies.

"He always has at least one case of the zoomies when I get home from work," I agreed.

"What are you wearing tonight?" Luna asked, and I slid a glance towards her.

"Why? Am I going on a date?" I asked, wondering what my attire had to do with a magick ceremony.

"Well, I suggest a loose maxi dress. No underwear."

Say *what?*

"Excuse me?" I asked, wondering just what I was getting myself into.

"Yes. This is real magick. We're going skyclad."

"You want me to get naked with you? Jeez, Luna, maybe take me to dinner and buy me a glass of wine first," I joked, but inside I was all *nope, not happening*. Easy for a white witch with not an ounce of fat on her body to casually dance around naked in the moonlight. When I danced, various parts of me jiggled. A lot.

And she says no drinks? Yeah, right. Like any self-respecting spring break student, I was going to need some liquid courage before I started prancing naked around a beach at night.

"So you're a comedian these days?" Luna winked at me.

"It's my night gig. Didn't I tell you?"

"I must have missed that between our late night conversations about Cash and Beau's new restaurant."

Cash. My heart tugged a bit as I thought about him.

"Don't even get me started," I grumbled as I made my way inside. "I'm going upstairs to find something that looks good with no underwear on."

"I'll entertain Hank," Luna called after me, knowing that now was not the time to get into a discussion about my sorta-boyfriend, Cash Williams.

He'd blazed into my life a month ago amid the mess of Luna being charged with murder, and had played knight in shining armor to my damsel in distress. It didn't hurt that he was a dead ringer for Channing Tatum and dropped phrases like "investment portfolio" and "second home." Beneath all that, he'd also turned out to be a pretty stellar guy and I'd found myself swept under by the pull that is all things Cash.

He'd been called back to Miami to investigate a string of break-ins at his newest club, and I'd only seen him once for a night when he'd come down to check in with Beau on his new restaurant, which Cash was an investor in.

Yeah, Cash invests in things. The only things I ever invest in are new packs of tarot cards and shoes, so there's that.

As men go, Cash was fairly good on the communication front and we'd kept in contact via daily text and phone conversations. I couldn't fault him for having been pulled away from our burgeoning relationship by his work. It was just crappy timing all around.

"Really crappy," I muttered as I yanked my closet doors open and perused my sizeable collection of maxi dresses.

It certainly didn't help that Trace, my best friend and dive buddy, had taken up with a girl who liked to wear neon scraps of fabric as a substitute for a bikini. Trace had stepped over the line of our friendship when Cash had moved in on me, creating an interesting love triangle of sorts. Though I'd been flattered, it wasn't as much fun to be fought over as the Real Housewives made it look on television.

And now Trace was living it up with Orange Bikini while I had a missing boyfriend.

"He hasn't even said he's your boyfriend," I reminded myself and yanked out a simple black maxi dress, made of soft linen that sort of flowed and skimmed over any lumps and bumps I might have. A shiver rippled through me as I thought about whipping the dress off under the stars.

Maybe telling Cash I was dancing around naked with other women in the moonlight would bring him hurrying down to Tequila Key to make sure I didn't suddenly switch teams on him, I thought as I discarded my underwear with a gulp and pulled the dress over my head.

Glancing in the mirror, I breathed a sigh of relief. The dress was voluminous enough to conceal the fact that I was wearing no underwear, and a higher neckline hid my ladies – which typically could never be without a bra.

"Luna, is it bad if I wear black?" I shouted down the stairs.

"Not if you want to summon demons," she called back.

I stopped short. Shit, I didn't want to call down evil spirits.

"Kidding," Luna called again.

"Thinks she's soo funny," I muttered and switched off the light before pounding downstairs, stopping at the base of the stairs with my arms wide open. "Here I am, in all my almost naked glory."

Luna gave me a once-over. "Perfect. Want to get a bite to eat before it gets dark?"

"Duh," I said, calling Hank and pulling a new toy out of my rotating drawer of toys for him. Hank came scrambling inside and huffed at my feet, his head cocked as he eyed the fuzzy banana in my hand.

Who comes up with these designs for pet toys anyway? I launched the banana across the room and Hank went scrambling across my wood floors in delight.

Luna waited by the door and I couldn't help but notice that she wore all white. I mean, she *was* a white witch after all, but here I was all in black.

"Are you Glinda and I'm the Wicked Witch of the West?" I asked, pointing between our dresses as we stepped onto my porch.

"More like the wicked bitch of the Keys," Luna sang out as she hopped behind the wheel of her white VW convertible with white leather interior. Did I mention that Luna does white well? I, on the other hand, don't think I actually own anything white, except a new maxi dress that I was going to try and gently break in.

It's the wine stains that usually get me.

"You're just cranky because you haven't gotten laid in a while," I grumbled as I climbed in her car, the black of my dress a stark contrast to the leather.

"Neither have you, if I might remind you?" Luna said.

The witch had a point.

Chapter Four

"DO YOU THINK Beau's at Lucky's, or working on the new restaurant?" I asked as we cruised in what could be called dinnertime traffic on a Friday night. Luna insisted on having the top down even though the heat was as one would expect for September in Florida. I slid a glance at Luna.

Her face didn't even glisten with sweat.

I could already feel my curls expanding in the heat, so I punched up the AC and glared at Luna when she glanced over at me.

"Okay, first order of business with this whole magick thing – I want you to write me up a spell that makes me impervious to the heat," I demanded.

"Oh yeah, like that's a thing," Luna scoffed.

"It's a thing. Look at you. Even your linen dress doesn't wrinkle and everyone knows that's virtually impossible. People keep insisting that linen is a great fabric but we all know it wrinkles the minute your butt hits the seat," I said, glancing down at my already rumpled dress.

Luna shrugged one shoulder and a corner of her mouth quirked up.

"I knew it! You do charm yourself," I said, slapping my palm down on the dashboard.

"Calm down, Diva. I'll teach you some glamour spells and whatnot as we get a little deeper into all this," Luna said.

"Yes!" I shouted, throwing my hand into the air, as we turned down the street with Miss Elva's house. "Hey, pull to the side and see if Miss Elva's on her porch."

Miss Elva is Tequila's Key's one and only voodoo priestess. A mountain of a woman, with sun-kissed brown skin, she smells like cookies and can curse a man at twenty paces. I loved Miss Elva just as much as I feared her.

"Think she's cursed Craig yet?" Luna murmured as she pulled to a stop in front of a weathered shake house with a wide porch. Miss Elva was sitting in her rocking chair in the corner, a caftan covered in a radiant red hibiscus print floating around her. She lifted a hand in greeting, a wide smile splitting her face. Ella Fitzgerald played softly from an old radio plugged into an outlet on her porch.

"Ladies," she called, her voice surprisingly melodic.

"Hey Miss Elva," we called, getting out of the car to climb her porch steps and lean against the railing. Miss Elva only had one visitor's chair on her porch, her message about overstaying your welcome loud and clear.

Miss Elva ran her eyes over my dress.

"What?" I demanded, shifting under her gaze.

"You're making her go skyclad?" Miss Elva asked, turning with a raised eyebrow to Luna.

"Damn it. I knew people would know I wasn't wearing any underwear," I complained to Luna.

"It's Miss Elva. She knows everything. You're fine, I promise," Luna rushed to reassure me, reaching out to run her hand down my arm.

"Child, I hope you know what you're pulling her into," Miss Elva warned.

"Miss Elva, come on now. You know she has magick. I'd rather she learned it from me than try something stupid when I'm not around," Luna said, her hands on her hips as she pleaded her case.

"Hmpf, I suppose so," Miss Elva said, turning a critical eye on me again. "How strong do you think she is?"

"Stronger than she realizes. She was able to break open cuffs and a door, and she clearly used your magickal pouch just fine, so I'm interested to see what else she's capable of. First she needs to learn to protect herself, though."

"You be careful with her. This one doesn't always like to follow directions," Miss Elva warned.

"Don't I know it," Luna said, huffing out a sigh and crossing her arms over her chest.

"Um, guys, I'm right here," I said, annoyed that they were acting like I was a small child.

They both ignored me.

"Will you be going to the Mabon Festival?" Miss Elva asked.

"I plan on it. I'll take Althea with me too," Luna said.

"I'll come with you as well. I'm not sure you two should walk into that alone."

"Why?" I demanded, "Aren't Pagans supposed to be peaceful?"

"Most Pagan groups are peaceful. Much of what they practice is kindness, harnessing the earth's energies, and honoring Gods and Goddesses. I have no quarrels with the Pagans. However, I don't like this Horace character."

"You know him?" Luna asked.

"I know of him. This is your warning, girls. Tread carefully with that man," Miss Elva turned her eyes on me. I swear she gave me an extra doubting look.

"I can handle myself, jeez," I muttered.

"And who didn't heed my warning last time something bad happened around here?" Miss Elva's voice rose. I hunched my shoulders and couldn't bring myself to meet her eyes.

"That would be me. But blame Luna, she got us into that mess," I said.

"Hey!" Luna said, smacking me lightly on the back of the head. We both snorted and laughter bubbled up.

"Speaking of, did you take care of Craig?" Craig was the reporter who had written that nasty article about Luna when she'd been accused of murdering her lover.

"He won't be working around here anymore," Miss Elva said, a small smile playing across her face, changing her expression from welcoming to sinister.

"Do I want to ask?"

"Let's just say that every time he tries to write an article, he can only type cuss words."

I was shocked – I had suspected something far nastier. And yet the curse was simple in its brilliance.

"So he can only write an article of swear words?"

"So long as he stays in Tequila Key," Miss Elva amended.

"I love you, Miss Elva," Luna said with a smile, bending over to wrap her arms around Miss Elva.

"I love you too, girl. But you need to come to me. We have some things to discuss. October is arriving soon," Miss Elva said.

Halloween. A big night for the undead. I wondered what Miss Elva and Luna might need to work on together, and then decided to push that thought from my mind. I had enough things to worry about.

"We'll come pick you up tomorrow?" Luna asked.

"Yes, let's go in the early evening, please," Miss Elva shifted in her chair and began to hum as the music changed to Howlin' Wolf.

"We'll be here," Luna said, bending over to kiss Miss Elva's cheek.

"Bye, Miss Elva," I said, wrapping an arm around her and inhaling her vanilla scent.

"You listen to Luna tonight, child. I don't have a good feeling about this," she murmured in my ear.

I pulled back to meet her eyes.

"Are you warning me?" I asked, searching her face.

"I'm telling you to listen to Luna." She clamped her lips together and began to rock in earnest.

"Everyone's always so damn cryptic around here," I muttered as I followed Luna off the porch.

"I heard that," Miss Elva called after me.

"I said I could use a damn beer!" I shouted over my shoulder.

"Child, I ain't raised yesterday," Miss Elva hooted with

laughter and I couldn't help but grin as I climbed into Luna's car.

As I said, Miss Elva is a favorite of mine.

Chapter Five

"AHH, TO WHAT do I owe the pleasure of having such beauties join me for an evening?"

I rolled my eyes at Beau but leaned over the bar and smacked a kiss loudly on his cheek. Beau was one of our best friends and completed our little trio. We were the perfect foil for each other, Beau with his steadfast manner and dry wit, Luna with her kind heart and on point observations, and me…well, let's just say that I added a little extra flavor to the group – if you can believe that a group made up of a psychic, a witch, and a gay guy needed any more flavor.

"We're just here for food, not drinks," Luna said pointedly as she pulled up a barstool. I rolled my eyes and shook my head slightly at Beau, indicating that he could ignore that particular order.

Lucky's Tiki Bar was the hot spot in a town that consisted of one main street winding along a rocky stretch of beach. Space was at a premium here and Fins, the local general store, jockeyed for position with the ice cream parlor and the nail salon. Beau had purchased Lucky's just out of high school with the help of an inheritance and had transformed it into the best restaurant in town with a not-so-secret after-hours gay club in the basement. Recently he'd acquired a new space at the other end of the strip, which he planned to transform into one of Tequila Key's only upscale restaurants.

"We weren't sure if you'd be here or at the new restaurant," I said as I sat down, happy that Beau still saved us our regular spots at the long circular wooden bar. The restaurant was packed, and a line of people waiting to eat straggled out the door.

"We're slammed this weekend so I need to be here. Construction is coming along nicely though," Beau said as he made our drinks behind the bar. When Luna was looking at her phone, Beau poured a healthy dose of rum into my mojito and I gave him a quick smile.

"We can't wait to come check it out," Luna said.

"Yeah, and doesn't your investor need to be here checking things out more often?" I asked, raising an eyebrow at Beau.

"You need to cut that man some slack. He's very busy, you know," Beau said, admonishing me for being annoyed that Cash hadn't been back to Tequila Key but once since he'd left for Miami weeks ago.

"Excuse me? I am also a very busy person, I'd like to add," I sniffed at Beau and sucked rum-soaked mojito through my straw.

"Busy being a pain in my ass," Beau said sweetly before turning to help a customer at the other end of the bar.

"Yeah, like I'm a pain in the ass," I scoffed, then turned to Luna. "I'm not a pain in the ass, am I?"

"Yes, but you're *our* pain in the ass," Luna said smoothly, studying the menu. "I think I'll go with the blackened tilapia."

Of course she would. My thoughts of a cheeseburger and fries were replaced with the sadness that was the salad menu.

"Sounds great. I was just going to get a garden salad," I said nonchalantly, flipping the menu over while Luna laughed at me.

"Why don't you get a bowl of chowder and a side salad? Something heavy and something light?"

"Good call." I reminded myself that I was about to be prancing around naked on a beach in a very short time. One less burger tonight was not going to do much for the extra pounds that would be bouncing around on the beach later, but women have a way of deluding themselves about these things.

I found myself reaching for my mojito again.

What's one to take the edge off?

"You need to not let those insecurities of yours kick in. Cash really does like you," Luna observed.

"Listen, I can't help if I'm weirded out by Cash not being around. He was all full court press and then poof! I've seen him once since then."

"And how was that one time when you did see him again?"

My thoughts flashed to a tangle of limbs in my sheets, my body glistening with sweat while I gasped for air and Hank hid downstairs.

"I suppose it went well," I admitted. Luna smacked her forehead.

"The man leaves a very pressing situation in Miami, spends forty minutes checking on Beau's restaurant – one in which he's invested heavily, mind you – and does not pass go until he's wrapped around you for the rest of the night. I wouldn't get too worried about this," Luna said, holding up a finger to signal Beau.

"When you put it like that..." I said, a blush creeping up my cheeks.

"What did I miss?" Beau demanded.

"Thea's convinced that Cash has given up on her," Luna said sweetly.

"Thea," Beau cocked his arm on his hip and glared at me. "We've discussed this. You're beautiful. The man is besotted. If you're going to have a hot man like that as your boyfriend, you'd better get used to him being busy. His world doesn't just stop because you waltzed into the picture."

"I don't even know how to waltz," I protested, smiling a bit when I saw Beau make me another stiff drink.

"You did a damn good impression of it when you danced around Trace's eager arms and landed in Cash's," Luna said, looking up from her phone.

"Hey now," I began, but Luna waved me off.

"Beau, can we get blackened tilapia for me, and chowder and a side salad for this one," Luna said, jerking her thumb at me.

"Really?" Beau raised an eyebrow at me.

"Yes, really." I shot Beau a glare. It wasn't like this was the first time I'd ever ordered a salad.

"Being all lovesick must have gotten to your appetite," Beau said, moving away to enter our orders on a computer screen.

"Remind me why we're friends with him again?" I said, crossing my arms over my chest. I was getting even more annoyed with where this evening was going.

"Free booze. And he's easy on the eyes," Luna said.

It was true. If I hadn't known that Beau was gay since, like, forever, I'd probably make a pass at him myself. His easygoing style struck a nice balance between high-end chic and casual surfer. It worked for him and – judging from the number of eyes, both male and female, tracking his movements in the bar tonight – it worked for a lot of other people too.

"Truth." I smiled at the server as he brought me my cup of clam chowder. I briefly wondered if I should have gotten a bowl, as Lucky's clam chowder was legendary. "So, one more time, run me through what we're doing tonight?"

Luna leaned back in her chair, crossing lightly tanned legs as she fingered the pentagram necklace that hung between her breasts.

"I'm going to teach you to cast a circle of protection. You'll generally want to use this when doing any sort of spellwork or rituals."

"Or what? I'll burn the town down or something?" I joked and took another swig from my drink.

Luna turned her blue eyes on me, her face serious.

"You could. Or you could summon bad energy. Or cause a spell to be visited upon you threefold. It's nothing to play around with."

"Then how come you let me do a spell without protection?" I asked, shoveling another spoonful of chowder into my mouth, not caring how hot the soup was.

"Because the breaking spell was a minor spell, and the intent was pure. Typically you're fine doing small kitchen-type magick like that. But when you start to get into rituals and bigger spells…a circle is needed."

"So what you're saying is not to get too full of myself because essentially the only magick that I've actually performed is akin to producing a quarter from behind someone's ear? Lovely, got it," I said, grumpy at the thought that my magick wasn't anything special.

Luna laughed softly and wrapped an arm around me to buzz a kiss on my cheek.

"Everyone starts somewhere, my friend. Think about the first time you had a tarot deck in your hand – it's not like you could have actually given a solid reading. Magick isn't like in the stories…you need to learn and build on your skills."

"You know I never liked school, Luna," I said, watching a grimace cross Beau's face on the other side of the bar. A rush of anger hit me and I sat up, cutting Luna off with a wave of my hand. Scanning the room, my eyes landed on the source of the emotion. I cut off a curse as I looked into the eyes of a nemesis of mine.

Theodore Whittier. The town know-it-all.

And it seemed he had company.

Chapter Six

"THEODORE'S OUT TO PLAY TONIGHT," I murmured to Luna. She leaned forward to look around me as Theodore made his way inside from the balcony seating.

"Who's that with him?" Luna asked.

A woman, clad almost entirely in pink with a fussy necklace made of some sort of beaded flowers and pearls, followed closely behind Theodore, her nose in the air. She gazed around the room in disdain; as though she was surprised she'd even allowed herself to dine among the common folk. Her closely cropped grey hair resembled a poodle, fresh and fluffy straight from the groomer, and the look on her face suggested she was one of those people who *always* asked to speak to a manager.

"Prude Whittier. The spawn's mother," I said out of the side of my mouth as Theodore approached us. I knew the moment he saw Luna and me, because his back stiffened, the wave of anger that hit me intensified, and he adjusted his bowtie, a nervous tic he had.

Well, at least I made him nervous.

The rum must have been kicking in, because I leaned back in my chair as they approached. Theodore was forced to stop or else he would have run into my shoulder.

"Theo, my man, great to see you again," I said cheerfully, Luna's snort behind me emboldening me.

Theodore grimaced, and my smile widened as Prudie sniffed and looked me up and down, taking in my tattoos and lack of bra. She grimaced in distaste, then looked away over my shoulder, refusing to acknowledge my existence.

"Ms. Rose. Boozing it up as usual, I see," Theodore said, moving to step forward and pass me.

Now *that* one hurt. I'd been known to enjoy a few cocktails on occasion, but everyone knows that psychics need a clear head to give readings. Three drinks was always my limit and I typically stopped at two.

"Are you implying something?" I asked sweetly.

"Theodore, let's move on. Away from these…people," Prudie said, tightening her hold on her tasteful black purse, as though we were going to jump her for her money.

"'These people'?" Luna asked behind me.

"You know…" Prudie said, making a circular motion with her finger by her head to insinuate that we were clearly lunatics.

"Crazy? What…is it my tattoos or my bright-colored hair that makes you think that, Prudie dear?" I asked, baring my teeth at Prudie. She stiffened, taking a step back.

"While both are regrettable decisions, it's satanic rituals and psychic powers that I don't hold with. Now, I must insist you let us pass."

"Right, you wouldn't want to be late for your board meeting, would you, Prudie? You look like a board meeting type. Theodore must get that from you. You two love handing out your opinions on things without actually having to do any of the work. I know your type," I said, surprising even myself with my words.

"Mother, now," Theodore ordered, grabbing his mother's arm and bum-rushing her past us as he shot daggers at us with his eyes. I turned around to see Beau shaking his head at me.

"What? Was that bad?"

"God forbid you ever have to apply for a permit or get approval from anyone who sits on a board in this town," Beau observed.

"I'm sorry. That *was* bad, I guess. But she just rubs me the wrong way. She wasn't being particularly nice to us either, what with calling us devil worshippers and all," I pointed out, annoyed that Beau wasn't immediately jumping to my defense.

"She was being a royal bitch," Luna agreed and I let out the breath I had been holding.

"Does that surprise you?" I asked, leaning over to take a mechanical bite of the salad I didn't really want. I wasn't surprised to find that my hunger had disappeared after my little spat with Prudie. Conflict typically upsets me and I usually avoid it at all costs.

"No. Not if Theodore is any indication of the type of spawn she produces. Just let it go. We can't do anything about the fact that they live in New Tequila. I mean, Port Atticus," Luna said, sticking her nose in the air and sweeping her hair over her shoulder dramatically. Her effort had the intended effect, and I felt the tension leave my shoulders.

"No, but trust me when I say that if either of them ever sets foot in our shop, they will be promptly removed." I turned and smacked Luna on the shoulder. "Hey! Maybe that's a spell you can teach me. A 'keep snobs away from me at all times' spell!"

Luna laughed and took a sip of her water.

"If I could bottle that spell we'd all be rich."

Chapter Seven

A FEW MOMENTS LATER, Luna hustled me out of Lucky's, barely giving me enough time to finish my mojito and wave goodbye to Beau.

"We've got work to do. I don't feel like being up all night tonight. Tomorrow's going to be a late one," Luna said as we moved past the line of people waiting for a seat for dinner.

"What's up with that guy?" I asked, pointing to where a skinny man, his blonde hair thick with dreadlocks, vehemently gestured with a stack of papers in his hand. The couple he was directing his tirade at moved nervously closer to the line, trying to discourage his ranting.

"Hey," I called out to the man, not wanting Beau's restaurant to get a bad reputation. "What's going on here?"

The man turned, and I looked into sea-green eyes – so light they almost disappeared into the whites surrounding them. I paused for a moment, reaching out with my mind to test the man's thoughts.

"Turtles?" I asked, raising an eyebrow at him, not bothering to explain that I'd just rifled through his brain.

"Yes! The turtles, man. They'll build over everything. Every last natural space. And the turtles will die," he hissed, his blond dreads shaking as he waved the papers in my face.

"What are these papers?" I asked gently, moving away from the line, drawing the sketchy environmentalist away from the nice people who just wanted some seafood for dinner.

"A petition! I'm trying to get enough signatures to stop the development of the condos over on the east side of Tequila Key," he said, shoving the papers at me with a pen in hand. His eyes were alight with the zealousness only found in true activists and myself when I spy a donut right around that time of the month.

"Aren't they starting work on that development this week?" Luna asked, tilting her head to meet Dreadlock's eyes.

"They are. That's why they must be stopped. No matter what," the blonde man seethed, hopping from one foot to the other in his worn leather sandals.

"I'll tell you what," I said, an idea forming in my head as I reached for the papers. "I'll sign your petition and tell you just who you have to talk to get this thing stopped. They're on the board of everything," I said, sliding a glance at Luna to see her biting back a smile.

"Really? Thank you," Dreadlocks breathed and I smiled brightly at him. Flipping the papers over, I held the pen in the air before I wrote down an address.

"Yes, of course, we all want to save the turtles. Okay,

their names are Prudie and Theodore Whittier. They pretty much control the town. Trust me, you'll know them when you see them. Think sweater sets and golf shirts," I said, smiling warmly at the crazy man. He nodded back at me, reaching out to put his hand on my shoulder.

Ice washed through me at his touch and my eyes shot to his face.

"You're one of the good ones. Thank you, Ms. Rose," he said softly, before rolling the papers and tucking them under his arm, strolling off to harass someone else on the street.

"That was odd," I said to Luna, reaching up to brush at my skin where the man had touched me. What was that weird wash of coldness I had felt from him? And how did he know my name? Making a note to bring it up to Luna, I followed her down the path to her car, my thoughts already jumping to the naked night ahead of me and moving past the odd encounter with Dreadlocks.

He certainly wasn't the weirdest person I'd met in Tequila Key.

Chapter Eight

"WHY CAN'T WE just do this in my backyard?" I grumbled as Luna's headlights flashed through the dark, illuminating a gravel road in front of us.

"Do you want your neighbors to look over the fence and see two naked women chanting around a pentagram?" Luna asked, her eyes on the road.

"It probably wouldn't be the worst thing they've seen," I pointed out.

Luna sighed and shook her head, slowing her car as we approached a bumpier part of the road.

"Hank would be a distraction. Distractions are not a good thing when casting a spell," Luna said, like she was explaining something to a third grader.

"Point taken," I said, then flinched when Luna switched off her headlights but continued to drive.

"Why did you cut the lights?" I stage whispered across the car. I could barely make out Luna's face as my eyes struggled to adjust to the dark.

"Because we aren't supposed to be on this beach and I

don't want anyone seeing my lights approaching?" Luna asked, again sounding as if she were talking to a third grader.

"Well excuse me if I don't go on naked night-time spell casting missions on the regular," I shot back, crossing my arms over my chest. As my eyes adjusted, I realized the light from the moon was more than enough to guide our way down the overgrown lane. As we drew closer to the beach, Luna swung her car to the side and began to execute a three-point turn.

"We leaving already?" I joked, my voice sounding entirely too hopeful.

"No, but I always like to leave my car facing out. You know, just in case," Luna shrugged and my eyes widened.

"Just in case of *what*?" My voice may have squeaked a little – I'll never admit to it, though.

"In case we need to get away quickly. When trespassing on a private space, you need to be prepared for anything," Luna said, quietly easing her door open and motioning for me to do the same.

I stumbled in the dark as I got out, and silently cursed myself.

Have a mojito or two, you said; it'll take the edge off, you said. My inner voice was thoroughly disgusted with me right about now.

"Here," Luna said from my side and I jumped.

"Damn it, Luna, you're like a cat," I swore, reaching out to grasp the velvet bag she was handing off to me.

"Sorry – natural grace, I suppose," Luna whispered, then motioned for me to follow her down the lane. Soft moonlight filtered over us, and I could hear the waves lapping against the rocks of the beach. The air – heavy with humidity even at this late hour – pressed thickly against my skin as I followed Luna down the rocky path, stepping carefully onto the beach.

Now, here's the thing about the Keys – you don't really get a lot of sandy beaches. In fact, most sand beaches are man-made by the resorts because it's what the tourists want. So when I felt my feet sink into sand, I grabbed Luna's arm.

"Is this a sand beach?"

"Yes, just a bit of one. There's a long rocky outcropping that kind of conceals this sandy part. That's why they're developing the new condos here," Luna explained, bending down to slip her sandals off.

I slid my feet from my flip-flops and stepped forward onto the sand, observing my surroundings. A line of palm trees jutted out from the rocky point, providing some privacy to the beach. Though the lights from town twinkled between the trees, we were essentially shadowed from anyone being able to see us.

"I can see why the turtles like this beach," I said, feeling a wisp of sadness sneak through me, knowing they would have to find another spot to lay their eggs.

"I know. It's really private – which I like. We'll have to figure out a way to preserve some of this land down the coast. I think Miss Elva and I should be able to come up with something that will at least protect a chunk of it," Luna said, and I beamed at my best friend.

I knew there was a reason I liked her.

"Well? Let's get naked," Luna said.

Did I just say I liked her? I lied.

Chapter Nine

"DON'T WE NEED TO, like, work up to that?" I asked, running my hands up and down my forearms as I searched Luna's face.

"Why don't we get a few things set up first, then?" Luna said, sending me a reassuring smile. I nodded, following her a little further down the beach. Luna turned a circle on the beach, then nodded to herself before using her toe to outline something in the sand. I drifted closer to watch.

"A pentagram?"

"A pentagram facing up, or north, in this instance. I'll finish by drawing a circle around it for our protection."

"Far out," I said and then clamped my mouth shut. Maybe two drinks and only a cup of soup – we all know I hadn't eaten that salad – hadn't been the smartest choice.

Luna pulled out what looked like white pillar candles from her bag and set them up at various points around the circle.

"Let's go, sweets. I don't know how much longer I can

delay this. Time to go skyclad," Luna said sweetly as she reached for her dress and pulled it over her head. I followed suit, closing my eyes and groaning softly as I whipped the dress over my head and dropped it in a pile at my feet.

Okay, so the night air felt kind of good on my naked skin. Maybe there was more to this skyclad thing than I had originally thought.

Steeling myself, I opened my eyes and looked over to where Luna waited patiently, her hands cocked on her hips, the moonlight making her skin seem to glow softly.

"This is a good light for you," I said.

Luna laughed and then motioned me forward so that I stood next to her outside the circle. She had several items in her hands, things I couldn't quite make out even when I squinted.

"So," Luna began and I forced myself to focus on her words even though I was a little lightheaded from the cocktails. "I'm going to teach you the correct way to cast a circle. There are abbreviated versions of this for when you're in a rush, but it's smart to know the full process first."

I nodded, motioning for her to go ahead.

"First I purify the space," Luna said, flicking a lighter on and making me jump. She held the flame to the end of an incense stick and the scent of frankincense filled my nostrils. Luna began to walk around the circle, tossing something from her bag into sand as she went.

"I'm sprinkling water and salt, and following the circle with incense. And I light each candle as I pass it," Luna explained as she poured water from a bottle into a small bowl.

"Why?" I said, then paused, slightly taken aback, as Luna shot me a look. I needed to know these things, didn't I?

"We are calling upon the elements for protection. Water is for water, incense is for air, candle is for fire, and salt is for the earth. This will help to strengthen our circle."

I nodded and waited for her to continue.

Luna bent to her bag, setting down the bowl of water and incense and pulling out what looked like a stick. I realized it was a wand.

"I will now cast the circle with my wand – please step inside," Luna ordered. I hopped forward, stepping close to the pentagram.

Luna raised her arms and I saw a low white light begin to pulse from her hands. Aiming the wand at the sand, she made one circular motion and for a brief moment, a circle lit up in the sand around us.

"Circle of power, I do charge you to be a sacred space and meeting-place between the worlds of the mighty and the worlds of man on a day that is not a day, in a time that is not a time, in a place that is not a place. Oh circle of power, I charge you to be a meeting-place of love and truth and joy…a strong rampart against all evil and harm, and a strong container for energy which is raised until we choose to send it out. In the name of the god and goddesses, I do consecrate you! So mote it be."

I shivered at her words, my nakedness forgotten as a hum of energy began to pulse around me.

"First you consecrate the circle. Then you invoke the elements," Luna explained. I nodded – surprised to find that a touch of energy seemed to brush against me – within me.

"I invoke the east, the watcher of the air," Luna intoned. I stayed quiet as she moved to the south for fire.

"I invoke the west for water," Luna said.

Just then my cell phone trilled from my bag and I jumped, startled out of the ceremony's atmosphere and ashamed that my own carelessness was interrupting Luna's lesson. Reacting on instinct, I stepped from the circle to reach for my bag to silence my phone.

"Thea, no!" Luna yelled at me.

A flash of light out on the water startled me and I watched in confusion as a wash of energy seemed to flow from the water into the circle. A huge plume of white smoke puffed out of nowhere, causing us to cough and wave the acrid smoke away from our eyes and mouths.

"Well, well, well! A lovely sight for my sore eyes," a voice crowed through the smoke. I squinted, unsure of what I was seeing, wondering if the drinks had been stronger than I'd thought.

Because sure as my breasts need a bra, there was a real life floating pirate, leering at Luna and me in all our naked glory.

See? This is why I don't play with magick.

Chapter Ten

"JESUS H. CHRIST," I swore. Well, kind of swore. A cuss if you're a Christian, I suppose.

"No, I am not He, but you may address me as Rafe," the pirate leered, his eyes drinking in my nakedness.

Rafe seemed short for a pirate, at least from what I could tell. Things got a little blurry around the point where his legs should have been meeting the ground and weren't. He wore a pirate hat – no eye patch though – and a white shirt open to the waist. Dark flowing hair and a broadsword completed the picture, and Rafe tugged on his beard as his eyes flitted between the two of us.

"Luna, what the hell?" I whispered to Luna, moving closer to her.

"You broke the circle while I was invoking water. You can't break the circle. Ever," Luna hissed at me. "Now we've pulled this 'Rafe' from the water."

"So send him back," I hissed back.

"I can't. You can only undo what's been done at the

precise time and moon phase. We need an entire month before the next almost-full moon cycle," Luna said angrily.

"Get. Out." My mouth hung open in shock.

"I will *not* 'get out,' not when I have two such beauties at my fingertips. Though I much prefer you, my curvy wench. A man likes to run his hands over a *señorita*'s soft curves when the nights are long." Rafe winked at me and I shuddered.

"That's it, clothes are going back on," I said.

"Stop. I have to close the circle," Luna ordered and I paused, waiting on her. My eyes followed Rafe as he floated around us, his delight in our naked bodies clear on his face.

"I give thanks, harm none on your way." Luna put her hands down and stepped back from the circle, eyeing Rafe.

"That's it?"

"I abbreviated. We have bigger problems. The circle is closed for all intents and purposes."

"A witch!" Rafe hissed and floated around to stare down at Luna. She straightened her back and looked up at him. I moved to her side, ready to do battle but not sure how.

"I am, at that," Luna said, never breaking eye contact with Rafe.

"In my day, you would have been burned," Rafe observed.

"Then I guess it's a good thing it isn't 'your day' anymore," Luna said. Her words were met with silence as Rafe considered her carefully.

"Fair enough, pretty witch. I will be watching you

closely, though. Now, introduce me to your lovely companion."

I groaned as Rafe winked and smiled at me.

"I am Luna, a white witch and one of great power," Luna warned, before throwing me a glance. "And this is Althea, a great sorceress who can see the future."

"A sorceress," Rafe breathed, floating over to hover right in front me, his dark eyes searching mine.

"Bang," I said, clapping my hands suddenly in front of his face.

"She-devil!" Rafe screamed and flitted across the beach.

Luna and I looked at each other and tried to contain our laughter. It was a wasted effort, though, and we were soon both doubled over, struggling for breath.

"God, Thea. Sometimes I just can't with you," Luna gasped.

"I'm sorry, I don't know what is wrong with me," I gasped back.

"You're going to get us in real trouble one of these days," Luna said, packing the candles and incense back into the velvet bag, since she was already bent over.

"Think he's gone?"

"I most certainly am not, daft wenches," Rafe said from across the beach, and I shook my head.

"So does he stay with us for the whole month or what?"

"I suspect he does."

The thought of Rafe hanging out with me for a month instantly sobered me.

"You take him."

"I will not. This is an excellent learning opportunity for you," Luna sniffed, and turned to me.

The hair on the back of my neck stood on end and I grabbed Luna's arm, yanking her to me.

"Don't speak," I ordered, closing my eyes and using my other senses to scan the beach.

A wave of malice rushed across the beach and hit me like a freight train, and I knew we had to get out of there. Something bad was about to go down.

"Run, now," I said out of the corner of my mouth.

And so we ran, the evil wave pulsing at me as we scrambled and gasped our way down the lane, trying desperately to be quiet. I bit down on my lip as the gravel dug into my feet and belatedly realized that I'd forgotten my flip-flops on the beach.

"My shoes," I whispered to Luna as we reached the car.

"Screw your shoes," Luna said, and I had to agree. They were just flip-flops. The passenger door wasn't even closed when Luna gunned the Bug down the lane, keeping the lights on her car off, bumping and careening recklessly around the curves.

"Was it a spirit?" Luna bit out, trying to focus on the road but desperately wanting to know what was going on.

"I don't know. Evil, just pure evil washed over me. I don't think it was a spirit but I just felt this impending evil."

"To us? Or to someone else? Do we need to call the cops?"

I thought about it for a moment.

"I honestly don't know. I don't think so…"

The new sheriff in town was one I actually liked, unlike the last one who had tried to kill me. You know, a minor detail. Chief Thomas had worked with the Coast Guard and was now getting his land legs beneath him as he took over patrolling Tequila Key. Though he was a fair and equitable sheriff, I just didn't know how to explain this one to him.

"Where are you taking me in this fine, strange chariot, ladies?"

Thank God Luna's windows were closed and she'd put the top up, because our screams would have woken the entire neighborhood we were now slowly cruising through.

"Rafe! You *cannot* do that to us," I exclaimed, turning my head to eye the pirate in the backseat.

"Do what? The witch told you I'd be around for a while. Well, here I am. Pretty lady," Rafe said, reaching out to run his hand down the back of my neck. I felt a light shiver over my skin and the softest brush of a touch, almost like a kiss.

"Hands off, buddy. I'm spoken for," I said hotly, craning my head away from him.

"We'll just have to see about that, won't we? I like taking things that aren't mine." Rafe looked at me, his smile wicked in his face.

"You've got to be kidding me," I groaned, burying my head in my hands.

"Maybe we don't drink and try to do spells," Luna said, her saccharine voice grating at me.

"Damn it," I said.

"Yeah, I can smell it on your breath," Luna said.

"Thanks, Mom. Got it," I grumbled. "Just get me home."

Luna leveled her gaze in the rearview mirror.

"Rafe, if you step a foot out of line with Thea, I'm going to banish you to the darkest corner of hell," Luna said, her bitch face in full effect.

"No need for such a threat – can a man not have a bit of fun?" Rafe protested.

"I mean it," Luna said as she pulled to a stop in front of my house.

"Wait, you mean he's coming with me? I thought you were just kidding," I protested, my eyes darting between Rafe and Luna.

Luna shrugged, smoothing her unwrinkled white dress.

"There are some things I can't control," Luna said.

"But, I can't have a ghost come live with me." I glared at Luna.

"Then perhaps you shouldn't have invited one in."

Maybe she had a point, but it wasn't like I'd directly *asked* for a ghost to come visit me. I wasn't summoning anything. It had been purely an accident.

"We're so fighting," I grumbled, grabbing my purse.

"No we're not. 'Cause otherwise you won't know how to send him back." Luna blew me a kiss and I sighed, knowing she was right.

Luna's always right. Though you won't ever hear me admit that. Well, maybe once in a while. But we can't have her getting a big head now, can we?

"Milady," Rafe intoned, bending at the waist and gesturing towards my door.

I shook my head as I moved to the door, wondering

just how I was going to put up with a lecherous pirate ghost for a month. "This is my life," I said out loud.

"At least you have one," Rafe quipped as I pushed the door open.

I couldn't argue with that.

Chapter Eleven

"WHAT. IS. THAT?" Rafe asked, hovering worriedly over Hank as Hank bounced around, sniffing the air below Rafe. Hair rose at the back of Hank's neck and he emitted a low growl. Astonishment washed through me as I don't think I've ever actually heard my happy-go-lucky dog growl before.

"He's a ghost hunter. You'd better watch out," I said and was rewarded when Rafe zoomed to the other side of the room, Hank racing across the hardwood floors after him.

Maybe there was something to this having a ghost around after all. If I could order Rafe to zoom around the living room all day, Hank would be all tuckered out by the time I came home from work. Mulling it over, I pulled my cell phone from my bag to see what call I had missed.

Trace.

I sighed and punched the button to call him back. I hadn't actually spoken with Trace in a while. Typically

Trace and I had a fairly set diving schedule, but with recent events we hadn't gotten wet in a while.

"Hey," I said, keeping my eyes on Rafe as Hank jumped onto the back of a red leather sofa and prowled after the ghost.

"Hey, how are you?" Trace asked, sounding distracted. I could hear a woman's voice in the background and was immediately annoyed.

"Oh you know, same ol' thing, you? Did I interrupt a date?" I tried to sound cheerful but suspected that I just sounded bitchy.

"Um, sort of. I just wanted to check if we were diving in the morning?"

My eyes went to Rafe again and then I thought about the Pagan festival tomorrow. I suspected I'd be busy in the morning with all the new people in town.

"I don't think so. There's some Pagan festival in town and I think the shop is going to be pretty busy. I'd like to get some sleep instead," I said, watching as Rafe reached out to try and pet Hank's head.

A sharp bark warned Rafe away and I huffed out a small laugh.

"You've got company as well, I see?"

Trace's words were polite but I could sense a current of bitterness below them. I sighed, wondering when we would go back to the easy friendship we'd once had, or if we ever *could* go back there. I missed my dive buddy, and my friend.

"Nobody important. Maybe Sunday or Monday we could do a dive?" I asked hopefully, knowing I could use some time underwater to clear my head.

"Sure, let's plan for Sunday morning."

"Deal. See you then," I said softly as a woman's voice called to Trace.

"See ya."

And that was just that, I thought, turning the call off and staring down at my phone, wondering if I should call Cash. I couldn't help but feel a little irritated by the woman's voice in the background. Trace was supposed to be into *me*. I rolled my eyes at that thought. What kind of woman was I turning into? I just wanted Trace to lust after me while I gave my attention to Cash?

I jumped when the phone rang in my hand.

Cash.

Well, then. Seems like my psychic powers were on overdrive tonight.

"Hey," I said softly, turning away from Rafe as a warm glow spread through me at his voice.

"Hey yourself. Did I catch you at a bad time?" His voice, which sounded like whiskey-soaked sin, reached to me through the phone and I realized just how much I missed him. Which made me feel even guiltier for having a brief lusty thought about Trace.

"Well, it's been better. But that's a story for when you're here," I said. Emphasis on *here,* I thought.

"That's why I'm calling. I think I'll be able to make it down at some point this weekend. What do you have going on?"

Hmm, how do I tell my investor boyfriend I had acquired a pirate ghost and was going to a Pagan festival to make sure nothing bad went down?

"Oh you know, this and that. Going to a festival with

Luna and Miss Elva tomorrow night, maybe a dive on Sunday."

"A dive? With Trace?" Cash's voice sharpened and I rolled my eyes.

"Yes, with Trace. He is the one with the dive boat, after all."

"That guy," Cash said, disgust evident in his voice.

"Calm down, Cujo. He's dating someone."

"Really? That's excellent news. I wish him much happiness," Cash said sweetly and I chuckled.

"Well, at least he gets to see her often, ahem," I said, wincing at the petulant sound that came through in my voice. A sigh greeted me through the phone.

"I know. I miss you, too. It was shitty timing for me to get called back to Miami. I think we have a lot of the problems with the club figured out, however, and I'm hoping to be back full time in Tequila in a few weeks. You'll have to help me look for a house," Cash said.

Well, now. How could a girl get mad at that? Hot boyfriend planned to come back soon and was buying a house, which translated to – he's putting down roots here.

Perfect.

"I'd love to help you pick out a house. I can chase out any lingering spirits for you," I teased.

"I plan on it," Cash said and then I heard voices in the background. "Ah, back to work. I'm at the club training on the new security system."

Now, normally most women would go into hyper-overdrive, trying to figure out if Cash was lying. Remember that whole psychic thing I have going on for me? It works great for situations like this, as I could read the truth in his words.

"See you soon," I said softly as we hung up.

"Your betrothed?"

My head shot up to see Rafe sitting on my counter, Hank pacing in circles beneath him.

"My betrothed? No, my boyfriend. Get with this century, Rafe. Speaking of…what's your story anyway?"

Well? If I was going to have a ghost hanging around I might as well get some background info on the guy. It was going to be a long month otherwise, if I couldn't figure out ways to drive Rafe crazy.

Rafe stood up on my counter so that I had to look up at him, his head disappearing into my ceiling. Reaching up, he pulled his hat from his head and executed a sweeping bow, made all the funnier for his head disappearing in and out of my ceiling.

"I am Rafe de Leon Rackham, captain of the great Santa Maravilla, the sweetest pirate ship in the waters."

"That's quite a name," I said, watching as he stood straight again, his head disappearing into the ceiling.

My stomach rumbled and I was reminded of the soup I had eaten earlier this evening. Grabbing an apple from my fruit bowl, I turned to the fridge and pulled out a hunk of Drunken Goat Cheese, my favorite. Adding some crackers and quickly slicing the cheese and apple, I soon had a little fruit and cheese board going. Uncorking an already-opened bottle of Rose wine in my fridge, I poured a glass and gathered everything in my arms.

"Rafe, why don't you get off the counter and come join

me on the verandah?" I asked, stepping past the counter where Rafe stood.

"That devil beast will accost me!" Rafe said, indignation bristling from him.

"He's a dog and he's a sweetheart. Maybe try being nice to him," I offered as I unlocked my patio door and slid it open, flicking the switch for my patio lights and large fans to go on at the same time. The heat had finally died down a little, though the ever-present humidity was just something you learned to deal with when living in the Keys.

I sat down on one of the couches, leaning over to place the tray on the low table and snuggling back into the pillow for a moment. Taking a sip of the cool wine, I let the impressions of what had happened tonight settle over me.

Leaving a circle while it's being cast or protected or whatever is bad. Got it.

Rafe poked his head out of the door.

Otherwise things can slip through.

Like Rafe.

I mentally played back the scene when I had felt that press of evil on the beach. Closing my eyes, I reached out with my mind to see if I could identify Rafe's energy signature. He was fairly easy to pick out, even with my eyes closed, and I would have known he was a ghost from a mile away. Which left me thinking that the wave of evil that had washed over the beach was not from the spirit realm.

And all too human.

I shivered as Rafe sat on the couch next to me.

"Don't be nervous, milady. I may look like a ruffian but I will be gentle with you."

I choked on a sip of wine and gasped for air, bending over as tears pricked my eyes and I tried to breathe. Gasping, I sat back up with a smile on my face.

"Okay, buddy, we're going to set some ground rules here."

"Ground rules?" Rafe seemed to be rolling the words around in his head.

"Ship rules? Captain's rules?"

"Ah yes, Captain's rules. That makes sense," Rafe said.

"This is my house. I am the Captain of this house. You must obey my rules."

"I'm not very good at obeying rules," Rafe said casually, picking something out of his teeth as he mulled my words over.

"Get good at it. Rule number one. Stop hitting on me," I said, popping a slice of cheese in my mouth as I watched him.

"I would never strike a comely wench," Rafe drew back, his eyes wide and horrified.

I swear this would be funny if it wasn't happening to me.

"I meant no sexual overtones. Or undertones. Or whatever you call it. Basically don't touch me, don't flirt with me, pretend we are just friends."

"Friends?"

"Yes, friends. No sexual innuendos. You talk about your day and your work. What your dreams are…that kind of thing."

"What if my dreams are about having my way with you?"

I glared at Rafe, a piece of apple in my hand.

"Nothing sexual. Period."

"Well, that's simply no fun," Rafe griped.

"Rule number two. You stay out of my bathroom and my bedroom."

"I can't watch you bathe?"

"Absolutely not. You must respect my privacy." I said, driving my point home by jabbing my finger into the air. Hank stood below me, his head turned toward Rafe, and sniffed the air.

"Fine, but you have to call off the devil-beast," Rafe grumbled, sneering down at Hank.

I sighed and patted the cushion next to me. Hank immediately jumped up and faced Rafe, his hackles raised once again.

"See? He hates me!" Rafe exclaimed, moving further away from Hank.

"Maybe he doesn't like some of the comments you've made about me," I said snidely – then I saw the very real fear in Rafe's eyes.

"Calm down. He's just a dog. Here, I'll introduce you two," I said, leaning over to pet Hank until his stance became less aggressive.

"Hank, that's Rafe. Be nice to him," I said, pointing to where Rafe sat. Hank swung his head between the ghost and me.

"It's okay. Really," I insisted, and Hank moved to where Rafe sat, sniffing curiously at the ghost as Rafe crossed his arms and looked up at the ceiling, biting his lip. When Hank didn't lunge at him, but instead sat and cocked his head curiously at Rafe, I smiled.

"See?"

"I can't believe you keep this animal in your home," Rafe said, though I saw he was shooting glances at Hank over his shoulder.

"Rafe, didn't you have any pets? Where are you from anyway?"

"We had a cat once. Before I left for sea," Rafe admitted.

"Ah, you're a cat person. Got it," I smiled down at Hank, offering him a piece of cheese. He took it from me delicately in his teeth and hopped from the couch to eat his snack in the corner.

"I'm not one for forming attachments. You really couldn't as a pirate," Rafe said, and I felt sadness wash over me as I thought how lonely that life must have been for him.

"You never knew who you would have to kill," Rafe finished eagerly.

Yup, sadness all gone.

"Rafe, I'm going to bed. Sleep downstairs, but stay out of the upstairs," I ordered as I collected my dishes and called for Hank.

"I don't know if I *can* sleep," Rafe wondered.

"Well, go do something useful with your time. But leave me alone."

Praying that the pirate would find somewhere else to go, I made haste to my bedroom, slamming the door and locking it behind me for good measure. Hank jumped up to his favorite spot on the bed.

"Hank, you're on ghost patrol."

And this is what my life has come down to, I thought as I stripped my dress over my head and pulled on a sleep tank. Ordering my dog to warn me about ghosts.

Never a dull moment around here.

Chapter Twelve

THE MORNING CAME WAY TOO FAST for me, and I groaned as I rolled over in my bed, pushing my hair out of my eyes. Hank bellied up towards me on the bed until his nose just touched mine, then gave me a swipe with his rough little tongue.

"Morning, buddy," I said, reaching out to scratch his tummy when he rolled over for me.

My thoughts were in a jumble this morning, as I tried to work out the impressions from my dreams last night. The most disconcerting one was that I felt like maybe I should have stayed behind to see what the evil thing on the beach was. I sincerely hoped our retreat wouldn't come back to bite us in the ass. Biting my lower lip, I hurried through my morning routine, pausing after my shower to examine my closet.

If we were leaving straight from work to pick up Miss Elva, I should probably dress for the day. Glancing down at Hank, I realized I would need to come home and let him out anyway, but still decided to grab a purple maxi dress from a hanger. The rich purple color complemented my lavender hair, and small gold sequins were sewn on the bottom half, giving the fabric a fun shimmer. Plus, this dress made me feel powerful – and I suspected I'd need to project confidence when we went to the Pagan festival later in the day.

Mulling over the potential for disaster to strike at the festival, I let out a screech when I rounded the bottom of my steps and ran face-first into Rafe.

"Jesus, Rafe. Don't do that," I shouted, holding my hand over my heart.

"What? You said not to come upstairs."

"So you waited at the exact bottom of the stairs?"

"Well, not all night. I watched some of the people in the box talk. Then I went out and about. But I figured I'd better come back and wait for you this morning, as I didn't want to miss spending the day with you."

I leveled a look at him as I crossed the room to open the back door to let Hank outside for his morning potty, leaving it open for him to come back in when he was finished.

"You don't have to stay with me the whole time, you know," I said, wanting to encourage separation in our spaces.

"We're friends. That's what friends do," Rafe said easily.

Oh boy.

"Rafe, where are you from? How come you don't have an accent?" I asked as I moved to where Hank was already doing a happy dance in front of his food bowl.

"I'm from Spain. I don't really know why I don't have

an accent. You sound strange to me. I don't know, maybe I picked it up from the people talking in the box," Rafe said, a puzzled look on his face.

"Weird," I muttered, gathering my purse and reaching inside Hank's toy drawer. Today's toy was a pirate, of all things, and I laughed a little, holding it up to show Rafe. He floated over to me, his brows crinkled in concern.

"What is this item? Is this a voodoo doll?" Rafe breathed, cocking his head to examine the toy's hat and broadsword.

"Yes, yes it is," I said solemnly, then laughed when Rafe gasped and moved back from the toy. "Just joking. It's a toy for Hank," I explained as I threw it to Hank and he chased it happily across the floor. Soon loud squeaks emanated from the pirate toy's head and Rafe had a horrified look on his face.

"I knew he was a devil-beast," Rafe hissed as he slipped out the front door behind me.

"He's not a devil-beast. Yesterday his toy was a banana. Don't worry so much," I said and then stopped short when I noticed a neighbor across the street looking at me oddly.

"Mr. Patterson!" I nodded and waved to him, then spoke through the side of my mouth to Rafe.

"Don't talk to me in public. People will think I'm crazy."

"I'm pretty sure you are," I heard the ghost mutter as he followed me to my bike.

"This contraption is your steed?" Rafe asked quizzically as I threw a leg over my beach cruiser and sat on the seat, putting my purse in the basket in front of me.

"Yes, and a most noble steed it is," I muttered as I kicked away from the curb, happy that I had pulled my hair back from my face as a low breeze, heavy with humidity, tickled my face.

Deciding that it was an iced coffee morning, I veered my bike from my road and towards the main strip in downtown Tequila. At 8:00 am, it was fairly bustling. Dive boats were pulling out of the harbor, while fishing boats were already long gone into the sea. Rafe chattered over my ear, exclaiming about cars and other things he found to be interesting, but I ignored him, seeing as how I had literally *just* told him not to talk in public.

I passed Fins, waving at the owner as he swept the porch, and pulled my bike aside to lock it in front of Beanz, the local coffee shop. Painted a pretty coffee bean color with turquoise blue trim, Beanz was the best spot in town for Blue Mountain coffee, straight from Jamaica. Luckily, Rafe kept his mouth shut as he followed me into the shop, the bell above the door tinkling with our arrival.

Wow, this place is packed, I thought, just as my eyes landed on Prudie Whittier holding court by the counter. Even the barista had stopped making coffee, her mouth hanging open in shock as she listened to what Prudie had to say.

"I'm quite certain it was witches. Well, you know the ones. After all, the dead body was found laid out on a pentagram. And we all know that potion shop is probably a bastion of witch activity. Wasn't that one girl in the paper just a month ago for murder? Lisa something?"

"Luna," I said loudly, causing a hush to fall over the

entire shop as Prudie straightened. Her lips were pressed thin as she surveyed me in disapproval.

"You're probably involved in this somehow," she observed and the barista gasped, her eyes darting between the two of us.

"Hey, Katy," I said, smiling at her as I moved through the room to stand in front of Prudie. "The usual, please."

"Uh, sure," Katy said, turning to retrieve the iced coffee from the low refrigerator behind the counter.

Hands on my hips, I moved forward another step, getting into Prudie's personal space and forcing her to take a step back.

"Now, why don't you tell me what's going on, Prudie? Because I'm quite certain I didn't just hear you accusing my best friend of a crime, as well as calling our business into question. Such an accomplished businesswoman as yourself would understand that's slander. I hope you know that I have some of the best legal counsel in the state, just a phone call away," I said sweetly, silently thanking my mother and her high-powered attorneys in my head.

"Well, I would never slander someone. Never," Prudie gushed, and I held her gaze, waiting for her to drop her eyes first.

"What happened?" I asked, crossing my arms over my chest. I caught a glimpse of Rafe hovering in the corner, but thank goodness he kept quiet as he took the scene in.

"Well, I just, I never…" Prudie exclaimed, warming up to her topic, "A body was found on the beach this morning, out by that new development. Laid out in the sand on a pentagram."

Shit.

Prudie looked around and lowered her voice, the effect forcing the ring of people around her to lean in to hear her words.

"And there were holes drilled into his head. With seeds imbedded in his brain. Other holes held little saplings, just sprouting. I heard it looked like he had plants growing from his brain."

A collective gasp rose from the crowd as people turned away, some covering their mouths, others reaching for their phones to get the gossip chain started. Prudie had chosen her spot well for dropping her gossip bomb. The news would be all over town in under five minutes.

"That's positively horrific," I said, and Prudie sniffed, nodding once to agree with me, while she ran her hands nervously over her pearls. I was still in her personal space, after all.

"It was just awful. The paving crew found him this morning. We're all just horrified, you know. Dead bodies aren't something we're used to around here." Prudie cast her eyes over me as though I was used to dealing with dead bodies.

Okay, so I've dealt with *one* dead body before. One.

"Who was it?" I asked, dread filling my stomach as my thoughts flashed to Beau, Trace, and Cash.

"I guess it was the guy who mixed up the tar? The pavement? Whatever it's called." Prudie waved that away. "Kurt something. He makes sure the asphalt is right before they lay it."

I couldn't help but feel a sense of relief wash through me, even though I felt sad for Kurt. He was bound to have had a family, people who cared about him.

"What an awful way to die," I murmured, nodding my thanks to Katy as she slid me a to-go cup full of iced coffee.

"I'll add it to your account," Katy said.

"Add a nice tip too," I smiled at her and she smiled back, clearly not thinking that I was the one who had committed the murder.

Taking a sip of my coffee, I turned back to Prudie.

"Now, you listen here, Prudie Whittier," I said, leaning in so close I could have kissed her. Her chest began to rise as she gulped for air, her myopic eyes all but bugging out of her head. The circle of people around us collectively held their breath. "If you so much as mention my or Luna's name around this murder, I will see to it that you never get to shop at Barney's again."

Prudie gasped and covered her mouth.

What can I say? I know how to hit them where it hurts.

"And that goes for the rest of you here. Most of you know Luna and me, and are customers of our store," I said, "and that includes your son," I added, turning to glare at Prudie. "We dedicate our lives to helping others. Remember that."

I pushed through the throng of people as Katy said across the counter to Prudie, "Leave them alone. It was probably the people at the Pagan festival, anyway. Sounds like an offering to the earth or something."

I would've slapped my hand to my forehead if I hadn't been holding an iced coffee in it.

I had forgotten the Mabon Festival this weekend in the rush of hearing Prudie's news. Granted, the murder didn't really seem like something that normal Pagans would do, but I wasn't so sure about ol' Horace.

That man screamed crazy.

"Let's go, Rafe," I shouted to the ghost, who was still hovering around inside. Startled, he zipped through the window and fluttered behind me as I aimed my bike toward the shop.

And tried not to let the niggling worry that I had forgotten something major eat at my stomach.

Chapter Thirteen

I ALMOST SPILLED my coffee all over my dress – I was moving at a dead run as I hit the front door of our shop. I stopped short when I saw Luna was with customers, though she darted a quick glance at me and shook her head once.

"Fine," I muttered, moving past a table of crystals and pushing the privacy screen aside to go into my shop. Flicking on the lamp in the corner, I patted my skeleton on the head before sitting down at the table and staring at my pack of tarot cards.

There was something I was missing here.

"Did you kill him?" Rafe asked companionably and I jumped in my seat.

"Rafe, you were with us last night. You know I didn't kill him," I hissed as the pirate sat in the chair across from me.

He cocked his head at me in confusion. "I know you didn't kill that one. I meant *him*," he said, pointing with his thumb to where my skeleton sat in the corner.

"Ohhh. No, that one's fake. Made of rubber," I explained, and Rafe immediately jumped up to go examine the skeleton. My screen moved as the front door chimed and Luna poked her head in.

"What happened? Did Rafe do something he wasn't supposed to?" Luna said, glaring over at the ghost. Today she wore what she considered color, a soft mint colored skirt that ran in a column to the floor and a white crochet crop-top that revealed a sliver of a tanned tummy. She looked cool, funky, and way more expensive than any outfit that I managed to pull off. See? That's why I stuck to maxi dresses. Pull it over your head and call it a day.

"No, Rafe's been minding his manners," I admitted, and Rafe shot me a grin.

"Yes, she-witch. Stay away from me."

Luna glared at him again, then crossed her arms over her chest.

"Talk. You all but ran in the door."

"There was a body – someone was murdered and laid out on the pentagram that we drew in the sand." The words rushed out, and I watched as Luna's eyes went huge in her delicate face.

"I'm sorry. Did you just say that a dead body was laid out on our pentagram?"

I nodded vigorously, sucking coffee through my straw with a loud slurping noise.

"I did. And he had seeds drilled into his head, along with saplings."

"No," Luna said, backing up a bit.

"You know what that means?"

"It's an offering. The seeds are meant to grow from the

brain, instilling the wisdom of the human into the universal consciousness of the world," Luna explained.

"How could you possibly know that?" I exclaimed.

Luna held out both hands in front of her.

"You can't know white magick without learning about dark magick."

"I told you she's crazy," Rafe whispered behind my ear and I flinched, turning to swat him away like an annoying gnat.

"And she also told you that I have power too. So watch it, Rafe," I said, menace lacing my words.

"This is not good," Luna said, beginning to pace my shop.

"Captain Understatement over here," I muttered, picking up my cards and beginning to slide them through my hands to soothe my nerves. The moon card fell out and my hand stilled over it. The picture was of a full moon, overlooking a beach. It took me instantly back to last night, and I shivered as I ignored the message in the card and slid it back into the pile. The moon card signified illusion and deception, showing that everything is not as it seems. Plus, the picture pretty much outlined where we'd been the night before.

"Death into life," Luna muttered as she paced, "Earth element."

Our eyes met.

"Horace."

The bell signaled a new customer on Luna's side of the shop, and I already knew.

"Say hi to Chief Thomas for me," I whispered, and

Luna shot me a look before slipping from behind my screen.

"Chief Thomas, I just heard," Luna exclaimed and I heard a low murmur of voices before Luna poked her head around my screen again. "You're wanted."

I shot a glance at Rafe, making a shushing motion, then crossed to Luna's side of the store. Lavender incense cast a soothing scent and a few candles flickered on a high shelf in front of a whitewashed wall. All was serene here.

"Chief Thomas," I said, greeting the new sheriff with a smile. He filled out his uniform well, and still radiated a boyish honesty that I found appealing.

"Althea, good to see you again. How have you been since…" his eyes darted between Luna and me, "the incident?"

"Fine. In shock for a few days, if we're going to be totally honest."

"And sad about losing the best sandwiches in town," Luna grumbled, causing a smile to flit across Chief Thomas's face.

"Yes, I know it's quite a loss to the town. Though Beau seems to be fixing the restaurant up nicely," Chief Thomas said. I could sense that he was stalling.

"I just heard about the murder, down at the coffee shop. From Prudie. Awful woman," I said with disdain, crossing my arms and leaning back against the counter. Not feeling even the least bit guilty, I took a scan through Chief Thomas's thoughts.

Shit.

Now I knew what had been bothering me. My freakin'

flip-flops! I'd forgotten them on the beach last night when we'd hightailed it out of there.

"Yes, well, she certainly knows how to get the news out quickly," Chief said.

"That has to be frustrating. What with you trying to catch the killer and all," Luna said soothingly, turning up the charm. I side-eyed her, but she refused to look at me, smiling sweetly at Chief Thomas.

"It certainly doesn't help. Gossip in this town spreads like wildfire," Chief Thomas grumbled.

"What can you tell us about the murder? Should we be worried for our safety?" I asked, deciding to take control of the situation and head the Chief down another path.

"Any time there is a murderer at large, you should be concerned for your safety," Chief Thomas said earnestly. I wanted to reach out and squeeze his cheeks. He really was too cute. I didn't want to tell him that bad people were always out and about.

"Absolutely, we'll be extra careful," Luna said, her voice syrupy sweet. "I really appreciate your coming by to warn us."

Luna can manipulate with the best of them too.

"Oh, good. That's good. Have you heard all the details then?" he asked, rocking back on his heels.

"Just some pretty gruesome ones from Prudie. Seeds drilled into the head?" I asked, raising an eyebrow at him in disbelief.

"Yes, well, that and laid out on a pentagram. Now...I don't want to go making assumptions here," Chief Thomas began.

Luna and I looked at each other and simultaneously put our hands on our hips.

Chief Thomas immediately raised his hands.

"I'm not saying you did it. I *am* coming to ask if you could shed any light on what this could mean. I'm, uh – well, I don't know much about devil worship and the like."

Devil worship. Really?

"So you think Luna and I are devil worshipers?" My voice went up an octave.

"No, no, no. Now, I didn't say that," Chief Thomas sighed and scrubbed a hand over his face. "Listen, you're the only ones I know in town who openly have a connection to this occult-type stuff. I just figured you might be able to help. That's all, I swear."

I picked his brain and found a rush of panic and sincere affection for us, so I gave Luna a look and we both backed down a little.

"Chief, there's a world of difference between good rituals and dark rituals. Thea and I are not practitioners of the dark arts. However, that doesn't mean that I'm not educated on them," Luna said. Chief Thomas's eyebrows shot up.

"You are?"

"I am. As I was just explaining to Althea, you can't know the good without knowing the bad. Otherwise how would you know what lines to never cross?"

"That's a good point. Makes sense when you explain it like that. So, can you offer me any information?"

"Do you have a photo?"

Both Chief Thomas and I looked at Luna, our eyes wide.

"Really? Ew," I muttered, rubbing my hands up and down my arms. I caught a flash of movement over my shoulder. Great, now Rafe had joined the group. I bet he wanted to see the picture too.

Wordlessly, Chief Thomas reached into the folder he was carrying and slid a photo out, placing it on the counter. We all turned to gaze down at the picture.

It wasn't pretty.

There was our pentagram, clear as day, though the circle wasn't visible, as Luna had cast it with her wand. A body was laid out, head facing downward from the point of the pentagram; dark sticky blotches stained the sand beneath his head. The man looked to be of Asian descent, a skinny man with tattoos snaking over his arms. Little seedlings poked out from his dark matted hair, making it look as if he wore some sort of leafy crown.

Seeing it in real life, even second-hand through a photo, made it seem even worse to me, and sadness washed through me as I thought about his friends and family. Instinctively, I reached out and brushed my thumb over his head in the picture, murmuring a quick Gaelic phrase.

"What did you say?" Chief Thomas had a suspicious look on his face.

"An Irish blessing. Sort of like a last rite. It's sad. Sad to see this. I don't know how you do this job," I admitted to him, turning away from the picture.

"That's two dead bodies you've seen recently," he pointed out.

"And hopefully the last," I said, meeting his eyes straight on.

Chief Thomas searched my eyes for a moment, then nodded.

"Luna? What does this say to you?"

"Well, the body is laid out facing downwards on the pentagram – which instantly signals dark ritual to me. I've only heard of the seeds in a body once or twice before. It's supposed to be like an offering to the earth, but this is usually done when an elder has died of natural causes. Or in this case, with the way the body is facing, I would guess it is an offering to an evil god; you can assume which one, though I won't say his name. The seeds growing from the brain though...that is kind of like a life-from-death cyclical offering to mother earth."

"The trees say new life to me. Growing from the earth – or from brain matter, in this instance," Chief Thomas said.

"Yes, new growth. New beginnings. Summoning of... things, you know...blood drained into the soil, gifts to the gods of below," Luna shrugged, raising her hands helplessly in front of her.

"Would these rituals be consistent with a Pagan religion?" he asked Luna.

"Not typically. Pagans are very peaceful. I follow some Pagan beliefs and rituals myself. Usually it's all about harnessing the energy for good, following the seasonal cycles, that kind of thing. It's typically a very pure sort of religion, one that's been around for centuries."

"I notice you've said 'typically' twice now," Chief Thomas observed.

Even I had missed that. Which was a reminder to me to

stay on my toes with Chief Thomas. His boyish good looks belied a sharp mind.

Luna shrugged lightly.

"Isn't it true that all religions have groups which break off and often become fanatical in their beliefs?"

Chief Thomas left that question hanging in the air for a moment before nodding his understanding. Picking up the picture, he slid it back into the envelope and turned to leave the store. We watched him in silence, Rafe hovering over his head, until he was almost to the door.

"Thanks, ladies. Oh – and one more question?"

"Yes?" Luna smiled.

"What size shoes do you wear?"

I froze, ice moving up my spine as I fumbled with the idea of lying to him. Deciding against it, I kept my face smooth and tilted my head at him in question.

"Nine and a half. Why do you ask?"

"Seven for me," Luna said quickly. Naturally Luna has dainty feet.

"No reason. Have a nice day, ladies. Watch your backs, please."

And with that Chief Thomas left the building, taking with him all hope that we'd get out of this scot-free.

Chapter Fourteen

"WELL, I'M SCREWED," I lamented, as soon as I saw his car drive away. Rafe swooped over and hovered nearby, twisting his hands nervously.

"Is that the local Hermandad?"

"The what?" I turned to look at Rafe in confusion.

"The – how do you say – keepers of the peace?"

"Oh, yes. We call them police now," I said, making a mental note to look up the Hermandad.

"Police, police, police," I heard Rafe mutter to himself as he zipped around the room, looking at items on various shelves

Ignoring him, I turned back to Luna.

"He knows about the flip-flops," I said.

"Well, yes, but unless they were some rare brand of flips, pretty much everyone in Tequila owns them," Luna pointed out.

I thought back to the pair I had been wearing. They weren't the cheapest brand, as leather was better in the heat of Tequila Key and wouldn't melt on the pavement like cheaper flip-flops did. Still, there wasn't enough to distinguish them from every other pair in town. I blew out a breath as the hammering of my heart began to slow down a bit.

"I think I'm okay. Unless I dropped something along the way."

"Did you?"

"I don't know! There was a lot going on," I said, my heart picking up speed again.

"Why don't you throw some cards on this?"

Luna had a good point. Being psychic was such second nature to me that I often forgot to use my skills to my own personal advantage. I pointed a finger at her.

"You may have redeemed yourself for dumping Rafe on me," I said as I crossed the room towards my shop.

"I knew I'd get back into your good graces somehow," Luna called after me.

"Let's see if you can stay there," I said over my shoulder as I stepped to a shelf tucked away in the corner of my shop. This was my shelf of personal instruments, things I used only for my own readings. I prefer to channel with items that only I have touched. Instinctively, I reached for one of my favorite tarot card decks, one featuring Boston terriers as the characters drawn on them. What can I say? I'm a sucker for Boston terrier-branded merchandise.

Instead, I found my hand hovering over my pendulum. A pendulum can be made of anything tied to a string; you use it by swinging it back and forth for the answers you need. My pendulum was given to me by my mother and featured a beautiful quartz skull at the end of a delicate chain. I loved my pendulum, as it always provided me with the answers I needed – good or bad. Pendulums are good for giving me yes or no answers, as well as allowing me to channel my energy so I could actually get a vision or two of the future.

"Ohhh, a sparkly skull. I love it," Rafe breathed from over my shoulder and I jumped.

"Damn it, Rafe, would you please not do that?" If I had been a cat the fur on my spine would have been standing straight up and I'd have jumped across the room.

"Sorry not sorry," Rafe shrugged, and I turned to glare at him.

"Excuse me? Where did you hear that phrase?"

"From the talking box. With all the people in it? A woman kept saying 'sorry not sorry' while another yelled at her. It was quite fascinating. Though in my day, women dressed like that were only found in the most indiscreet of places. If you get what I'm saying…" Rafe leered at me, his eyes sparkling with delight.

"Rafe, were you watching Shahs of Sunset on Bravo TV?"

"Ah, yes. I think that was the name. Then they kept flashing some sort of lines crossed over each other in a square with the words 'sorry not sorry'."

That stumped me for a second, then I smacked myself in the forehead.

"Hashtag sorry not sorry." I just shook my head. How could I explain to a ghost the direction our society had taken in the past few hundred years? This was his first time seeing a television. I wasn't about to try explaining Twitter or the Internet to him.

"Rafe, go bother Luna. I need some alone time, please."

"But I want to watch you do magick."

I blew out a breath and counted to five. Who actually counts to ten anyway? Meeting his eyes, I reached out my hands as though I was going to push him away.

"Go. Away. Now."

"Fine," Rafe flitted away while muttering something that sounded suspiciously like "Bitch has an attitude." It appeared I would need to restrict his television viewing. Maybe I could install one of those programs on the television that forced him to watch only educational shows. Bravo TV probably wasn't the best slice of society I could expose him to.

Okay, I admit: I love Bravo. But only because I'm a student of human nature.

I swear.

Sitting down at my table, I pulled a small notepad from my drawer along with a pen. I began to sketch a diagram that would help interpret the pendulum's movement. But instead of just the typical yes/no answers, I also added a square with a number on each side and a compass in the middle.

Closing my eyes, I held my pendulum over the paper for a moment as I thought about the question I wanted to ask.

"Are we in danger?"

I breathed deeply and cleared my mind, allowing myself to be open to the universe. In a matter of moments, I opened my eyes to see my pendulum swinging decidedly in the direction of my YES sign.

"Lovely," I muttered.

"Will someone else die?"

Closing my eyes, I tried to clear my mind again but gasped this time when I got a flash of Rafe streaking across a moonlit beach and Miss Elva bellowing to the moon. When my eyes popped open, I saw the crystal skull circling the number two, signaling that there would be another death. The morbidity of the skull and the vision of another death on the beach sent a shiver through me as I tried to hone in on more details of my vision.

"Find out anything?"

Rafe popped in the room and the vision slipped from my mind. I glared at him and he floated backwards, his hands raised defensively.

"Women in my day knew not to talk back to their men," Rafe said.

"Good thing you're not my man then," I retorted, closing my notebook and pushing away from my table.

"I don't see any man claiming you," Rafe pointed out.

"Rafe! Get out!" I all but shouted. I was annoyed with Rafe, scared from my vision – and frustrated by the grain of truth in Rafe's words.

Even though Cash had been consistent with his communication, I had to admit that I missed him. And that I was worried our budding relationship wouldn't be able to manage distance like this when we were just starting out.

Shaking my head, I shoved those thoughts aside. I had bigger things to worry about.

"Luna," I called.

Luna stepped into my room, her eyebrows raised in question.

"There's going to be another death."

Chapter Fifteen

I SOMEHOW MANAGED to make it through my client readings that day, though my anxiety was beginning to kick up a notch. I was starting to think going to the Pagan festival would be an exercise in poor judgment.

"How'd it go today?" Luna asked, having closed down her side of the shop already. She leaned against my wall, a white suede purse thrown over her shoulder.

"A lot of people trying to contact their dead pets. The universe is teaching me a lesson," I grumbled. A month or so ago, I had quickly answered a client's question about her deceased show cat, and had put her at ease that her beloved Bitsy was doing well in the afterlife. Though it had been a teensy white lie, at the time, I'd felt no moral issues with it. It seemed as though the word had spread and now I was trying to pick up energy traces of deceased pets on the regular. Again, universe, I hear you, loud and clear.

"I'm sure the novelty of that will pass and you'll get back to reading regular clients again soon," Luna soothed.

"I certainly hope so," I said as I tidied my table and

then reached for my purse. I met Luna's eyes as I crossed the room. "Are you sure we should go to this festival?"

"I think we need to get a better read on Horace. I honestly don't think this is going to be like any Pagan festival I've ever been to. Which worries me…I'm not sure what kind of rituals he will be invoking."

"Sweet, more rituals. Super excited about that," I said as I pushed through my door and held it open for Luna.

Luna smiled at me, her expression as peaceful as could be.

"You get used to it. Sure, the word 'ritual' can be a little scary, especially after our experience last night, but not all rituals are bad. If you wanted to get down to the nitty gritty of it, Christians use ritual when they have you drink the 'blood' of Christ during communion. So, you know, it all depends on the setting and the intention," Luna explained as she walked to her car.

"That makes sense. But Horace creeps me out," I pointed out as I hopped on my bike. "Hey, where's Rafe?"

"I told him there was a nude beach on the other side of town," Luna shot me a grin before she got behind the wheel of her car.

She's a smart witch.

I pedaled toward home, trying not to let my anxiety get the better of me, and tried to work through the vision that had come to me earlier in the day. So far as I could see it, as long as I kept us all away from that beach, we'd stay out of trouble.

I slowed to a stop when I rounded a corner and saw the dreadlocked environmentalist from the night before. He wore the same outfit as yesterday and his dreadlocks were all but flying as he pointed angrily at Prudie Whittier's shocked face.

Would it be small of me to laugh?

I smiled, watching as Prudie crossed her arms and shrank back as Dreadlocks shoved papers in her face, pointing at something on the paper. Deciding to move on before they saw me, I pushed my pedals down and left them behind me.

Who knows? Maybe Prudie would actually do some good in her life and help protect the turtles on that beach.

Pulling up to my house, I saw Hank's ears poke over the windowsill. How did he always know when I was coming home? I briefly wondered if Hank was also a psychic before I opened the door to his barks of joy.

"Hey buddy," I said, bending over to pet him before he raced across the room to find a toy to bring me.

"Let's get you outside," I said, knowing we didn't have much time before Luna would be here to pick me up. I opened the door for Hank, letting him race out into the backyard, while I considered whether I needed to change for tonight.

What does one wear to a Pagan festival, anyway?

Figuring the maxi dress I was wearing would be fine – I paused to think about shoe options. Wondering if there would be any chance of us needing to make a run for it, I slipped out of my flip-flops and slid my feet into a pair of Toms. Even if they weren't the best with the dress, I knew I could run in them.

"Hey," Luna said, poking her head in the door. I paused, my mouth dropping open as I took in her outfit.

She looked like a goddess. Threads of silver ran

through the white robe that floated around her, while a nude bandage dress fitted her like a second skin, creating the illusion that she was naked under the robe. A huge statement necklace dripping in crystals hung around her neck, and she'd woven a sparkly crown through her hair.

"Um, should I bow?" I asked and Luna laughed, before doing a little twirl that sent the robe flowing out around her in a graceful arc.

"Festival garb. I love it," Luna admitted.

"Well, now I just feel underdressed," I said, holding up a Toms shoe in one hand.

"Hmm, those certainly are...serviceable," Luna said, one perfectly groomed eyebrow arching in dismay as she examined my choice of footwear.

"I just figured I'd better have good shoes on in case we needed to run," I admitted.

Luna shrugged.

"Maybe. But I think Miss Elva and I can manage any danger. Honestly, I swear you forget your friends are magick. And that you're magick too," Luna said pointedly.

"Well, excuse me, I'm new to the magick thing," I said, sliding the Toms on my feet anyway. What did I care? It wasn't like I had anyone to impress at the festival. "Do I need to change?"

Luna looked me up and down, then shrugged.

"What is that supposed to mean?" I asked, hands on my hips.

"I mean...it's a festival," Luna said slowly, like she was explaining something to a child.

"I get that. What's wrong with the maxi dress?"

"If you want to draw attention to yourself, it's fine,"

Luna said, bending over to retrieve and throw a toy that Hank had dropped at her feet.

"I'm the one who'll stick out?" I asked, pointing my finger from her ensemble to my dress.

"Oh yeah. For sure," Luna nodded.

"I knew this was going to be a thing. Now it's a thing," I complained as I went upstairs, racking my brain for anything dramatic I might have in my closet.

I dug through my closet until I found a gift that my mother had sent me from Greece. Or Indonesia; I could never be sure with her. It was a flowing caftan in a screamingly bright floral print of red and purple, with coins dangling from the sleeves so that I jingled when I walked. I'd actually worn it with a turban one year when I dressed as a psychic for Halloween, and the outfit had been perfect.

Sighing, I slid my dress off and pulled the caftan over my head, the cool silk fabric brushing softly against my skin. Turning, I checked myself out in the mirror.

Okay, so maybe there's something to this whole caftan thing. It was breezy, it flowed around my body, and I'd be able to run in it if needed. I moved my arms and the coins gently tinkled, a charming sound if I was forced to admit it.

"Fine, caftan it is. But I'm not wearing a crown," I muttered as I moved to my jewelry stand and pulled a necklace – chunky amethyst stones with a Celtic protection knot in the middle – from a hook.

One could never be too careful.

Pulling the necklace over my head, I fluffed out my

curls and made my way downstairs, the tinkling of my caftan signaling my approach.

"Much better," Luna said, nodding her approval. "I fed Hank. Are we ready to go?"

"What are *we* going to do about food?"

"They'll have food there."

"Great. It better not be something weird like pig's ear," I complained, as I pulled out a fresh toy for Hank and tossed it to him.

What? A girl's gotta eat.

Chapter Sixteen

"TALK TO TRACE LATELY?" Luna asked on the way to pick up Miss Elva.

"Who's Trace?" Rafe asked from the back seat. He'd shown up just as we were leaving, seriously miffed that Luna had sent him on a wild goose chase to see some naked ladies.

"Oh, you're talking to me again?" Luna asked.

"Maybe," Rafe sniffed, angling his head away from Luna.

"Trace is one of Thea's best friends. And he has a crush on her. She kind of has a crush on him, too. But instead, she's chosen the sexy, wealthy investor who also makes her blood boil. It's tough being Althea," Luna said dryly and I smacked her on the shoulder.

"Don't make me rip this cloak of yours," I grumbled.

"What is an investor?" Rafe asks.

I glanced at Luna before answering. "Well, basically an investor gives money to businesses and then when the businesses become profitable, they return the money with interest. More or less."

Rafe nodded seriously. "And what does this Trace do?"

"He runs a scuba diving boat."

"A captain of his own boat? Why, you must choose him," Rafe said excitedly.

Of course the pirate would tell me to go with the seafaring man.

"It's not that simple," I said, rolling my eyes at Rafe.

"In my day, I just took who I wanted. It was *quite* simple," Rafe said, leering down the V-neck of my caftan.

"Guess we're lucky it isn't your day anymore," I said, tugging my dress higher up.

"Those were good times. Plundering, pillaging, taking captives. People are so polite here," Rafe observed.

"You mean they're decent humans?" Luna asked.

"Who says I'm not decent?" Rafe demanded.

"Well, you pretty much try to sexually harass Althea and I every chance you get," Luna pointed out.

"I would think two such beauties as yourselves would enjoy that," Rafe said, honestly confused.

"I think he just complimented us," I said to Luna.

"Yeah, he's trying to flatter me into not banishing him," Luna muttered as she pulled to a stop in front of Miss Elva's house.

"Should we get out?"

"Yes, let's go up there. I don't want to spring Rafe on her in the car," I said.

"Do you think she'll even be able to see him?" Luna asked.

It was true. Most people couldn't see ghosts. Luna and I had that extra fun ability.

"I guess we'll have to see."

We all got out of the car and made our way to Miss Elva's porch. The sun hung low in the sky – just kissing the horizon – but the heat was still present per usual. The sky was clear and a light breeze kicked my caftan up. A good night for full moon festivities, I thought.

"Whoa," I breathed, stopping on the stairs as Miss Elva stepped from her weathered front door.

Her outfit put mine and Luna's to shame. A sequined turban with peacock feathers sticking easily a foot in the air was perched on her head. A fully beaded and sequined cloak in a rainbow of colors flowed around her large body, shimmering and shaking with her movements. She looked like that moment when the sunlight hits the water and explodes in shimmering diamonds.

"Praise the Lord for delivering such beauty to me," Rafe crossed his chest.

"You're Catholic?" I whispered, but he ignored me, his enraptured gaze focused on Miss Elva.

"Well, now. What have you brought me?" Miss Elva demanded, her hands on her hips as she surveyed Rafe. Rafe floated over to her and my jaw dropped as he took his hat off and bent at the waist, delivering a sweeping bow to Miss Elva.

"I am Rafe de Leon Rackham, head of the great Santa Maravilla, the sweetest pirate ship in the waters. And never have I been presented with such beauty in my life. I implore you to allow me to love you," Rafe said, and Miss

Elva's cloak shimmered with movement as she let out a belly laugh.

"I thought he just pillaged his lovers," I whispered through clamped lips to Luna. She just shook her head as we watched the spectacle unfold.

"Well, I'll be damned, you've got yourself quite the rake here," Miss Elva said, batting her eyelashes at Rafe.

"Did she just bat her eyelashes?" Luna whispered.

"I'm *your* rake," Rafe insisted, his eyes drinking in all that was Miss Elva.

"Sho enough, you've got a naughty one on your hands," Miss Elva slapped her leg and laughed her big laugh. Turning to us, she smiled. "Where'd you find this one?"

I opened my mouth to explain, but Luna cut in.

"Someone over here likes to drink before trying to cast a circle," Luna said. I poked her in the side.

"Knock it off," I whispered.

"Child, didn't I tell you to listen to Luna?" Miss Elva said, her tone implying I was a total idiot.

"Yes," I sighed, "you did."

"And did Luna tell you that you could drink before doing a ritual?" Miss Elva said, hands on her hips, Rafe hovering around her in rapture.

"No," I said meekly.

"And what made you think you could disobey that?"

I threw my hands up. "I'm sorry, okay? I got it. Listen to Luna. Listen to you. No drinking before spells. Don't you think I've learned my lesson? Rafe is punishment enough."

Rafe drew back, looking offended.

"I like him," Miss Elva declared, and Rafe immediately went back to fawning over her.

"And I like *you*, my great queen," Rafe said.

"What are you doing with him?"

"He's going back at the next cycle of the moon," I said.

Miss Elva turned and surveyed Rafe.

"I think I'll keep him."

"Oh, my beauteous lovemountain, I will do anything for you," Rafe gushed, floating around her in dizzying circles.

Miss Elva chuckled deep in her throat and I just shook my head, turning to look at Luna.

"Can she have him?"

"By all means," Luna said, and Rafe crowed in delight.

"It's like he's a lost puppy or something," I muttered as we made our way down the steps to Luna's car. I slid into the small back seat, knowing Miss Elva would need the room of the front seat. Rafe squeezed next to me, his presence cold against my skin whenever he brushed against me. His eyes were focused adoringly on Miss Elva.

"Rafe, I thought you loved *me*," I said, deciding to poke the bear a bit.

"I lusted after you. I like your curves. But I love Miss Elva. She's more woman than you'll ever be," Rafe scoffed and I drew back, stung a bit.

"Rafe, that's unacceptable. Just because not all women are as powerful and full-figured as I am doesn't mean you can be mean to them. I don't tolerate such nonsense around me. We celebrate *all* women's beauty," Miss Elva scolded.

Rafe looked like she had kicked him. "Sorry, Althea," he said, his head hanging.

"I get it," I said, deciding to be nice. "We all aspire to be Miss Elva one day."

Her laughter all but shook the car and I couldn't help but grin as we zoomed through the streets of Tequila Key towards the outskirts of town. But as we left the main road, a wave of nervousness washed through me.

"You calm down back there. Everything's going to be just fine," Miss Elva said, her voice authoritative.

Famous last words.

Chapter Seventeen

IN MOMENTS, WE'D approached a turn off the main road. Had there not been a small sparkly marker of sorts, I wouldn't have noticed the turn. Luna eased the car onto the gravel road and we all fell silent as we followed the road between overgrown bush that concealed our view ahead. Luna eased off the gas a bit as we crunched along through a turn and our view opened up.

Illuminated in the headlights were two folding tables pulled at odd angles across the road, effectively blocking our path as we neared. Beyond the tables, what looked like a tent city was spread out, a cacophony of colors and movement. The scene made me think of a circus performers' village. Lines of smoke from various fires streamed into the sky, while a woman – naked but for long ribbons tied around her wrists – pirouetted by.

"Toto, we aren't in Kansas anymore," I murmured and Miss Elva snorted.

"Now child, everyone's religion looks a little different.

The Pagans like to celebrate. No need to judge," Miss Elva said.

"No judgment," I said as a man riding a bicycle with a Bill the Cat doll firmly lodged on the handlebars weaved between the two tables, raising his hand to wave at the men sitting there. Luna eased the car to a stop and rolled down her window.

"Evening, gentlemen," Luna said, her charm at a ten.

"Ma'am." A bristly bearded man wearing a lavender tank top and plaid shorts nodded at Luna from his seat.

"We've been invited by Horace, though we haven't paid any pre-registration fees," Luna said.

"You have to pay registration fees?" I asked.

Miss Elva turned around and nodded solemnly at me, her dark eyes knowing.

"The Pagans are very organized, you know. There's a registration table, classes, healing booths, vendor booths, a nightly ritual, and an opening and closing ceremony. It's all very well run."

"This is far more organized than I was expecting," I admitted.

"Would do you some good to poke your head outside that bubble you live in," Miss Elva remarked. I stuck my tongue out at the back of her head.

"I saw that," Miss Elva said.

I shut my mouth as the bearded man approached our car and peered in, his eyes taking in Miss Elva's outfit before settling on me.

"What's her story?" he asked, motioning towards me with his clipboard. Oh sure. Miss Elva and Luna don't get questioned, but I do. Figures.

"She's an esteemed psychic and tarot card reader," Luna said smoothly.

"Oh, right. She was going to come give us readings," the man brightened.

"Ah, but I forgot my cards," I said, holding my hands up in a too-bad motion.

"Sorry not sorry," Rafe whispered beside me and I had to bite the inside of my cheek to keep from laughing.

"That's okay, plenty of decks around here. If Horace invited you, you're fine with us," the man said, stepping back from the car. "You're alright to go. Just park your car in the lot to the right here."

"Thank you," Luna called and drove the car to the lot, squeezing the Bug into a tiny spot near the front. "Easy getaway."

"You worried about something, Luna?" Miss Elva asked as she hauled herself out of the car.

"Althea is."

"What's on your mind, girl?" Miss Elva asked.

I shrugged one shoulder, scanning the near-empty parking lot before turning to look at Miss Elva.

"There's going to be another death. And I got a flash of you and Rafe on the beach, doing some sort of crazy magick."

Miss Elva patted me on the shoulder.

"Don't you worry your own mind about this stuff, honey. These things often take care of themselves."

"That's what I'm worried about."

"It isn't time for worry. For now, we celebrate the Autumnal Equinox." Miss Elva said with a small smile.

"Did Luna tell you about Horace?" I asked, falling into

step beside Luna and Miss Elva as we made our way through the parking lot and towards the tent city.

"Yes. Said he's a radical. That she doesn't trust him."

More or less. I nodded, deciding it was probably best not to talk about Horace as we entered his domain.

And what a domain it was. Once we'd begun our trek into the tent city, I was able to see that there were some clearly defined areas set up. It was easy to see the vendor area, as long tables were stretched in front of various sized tents, each table boasting goods ranging from crystals to oils to knives, staffs, and wands. Pretty much what you would expect at a festival like this.

I eyed a group of topless women sitting on the ground, chanting and playing hand-drums. I noticed that Rafe didn't give them a second glance; he only had eyes for Miss Elva. Maybe it really *was* love. Because by my estimation these women were well-endowed. Even I was impressed.

I could see now why Luna hadn't wanted me to wear something basic. The fashions here ranged from scantily-clad women and men covered in body paints to full-on regalia. I'm talking cloaks, head pieces, and layers of crystals and jewelry.

We passed a group of teenagers sitting on the ground, listening intently to a woman clad in a crushed velvet cloak of cerulean blue. She was gesturing to a whiteboard with the words "Ritual Construction" labeled at the top.

"Althea should join that class," Luna muttered and Miss Elva snorted.

"They have classes?"

It hadn't occurred to me that I could take a class in

ritual construction, and I had to admit I was a little intrigued.

"Festivals typically have all sorts of classes. Psychic self-defense, aspects of the goddess, ritual constructions, raising Pagan children, all kinds of things. It's a way to keep the religion going as well as offer more formalized instruction," Luna explained.

"So, all in all, does this seem like a fairly normal festival to you?" I asked as I watched a man with glittery ram horns glued to his forehead wander by.

"Actually, it does. It's a nice mix of people having fun, people taking things seriously, and a slew of vendors and workshops. Perhaps a little more nudity than usual, but even that isn't *that* far out of the realm of normal. Pagans are a fairly earthy and accepting sort. All in all, I'm impressed so far," Luna said.

"Well, I'm certainly glad to hear that," a low voice sounded over our shoulders, and we all turned at once.

Horace stood before us, naked to the waist, a loincloth tied loosely around his privates. A ritual cloak, looking to be made out of some sort of green woven material which alternately gleamed and sparkled, hung loosely from a crystal-embedded cord around his neck. He wore the same soft leather boots I had seen on him the other day, and his white hair flowed from beneath an intricate crown made of small bones ending in huge horns, rising easily a foot above his head. His horns were higher than Miss Elva's feathers, and I could tell immediately that she was miffed.

"The devil!" Rafe hissed in my ear. I did my best to pretend I hadn't heard him.

"Horace," Luna said, by way of acknowledgement.

"Luna, Althea. Lovely to see you could make it. I was beginning to think you wouldn't show. And yet, here you are. Along with this radiant creature," Horace purred, his odd-colored eyes landing on Miss Elva's robes.

"I'm all female, thank you very much," Miss Elva said, and Horace laughed softly.

"Of course, my apologies. What is it you do then?" Horace watched Miss Elva closely.

"Clerical work," she replied smoothly.

Miss Elva was as much somebody's secretary as I was a Supreme Court Justice, but we all allowed that one to slide as we watched Horace for his response.

"Interesting. I'm sure there's a need for it here," Horace replied, running one hand lightly up and down a large wooden staff he carried.

"It pays the bills," Miss Elva quipped, and I almost smiled.

"Indeed. Well, you've shown up a little late, Althea. I'm not sure if you'll have time to give any readings before our ceremony."

Oh darn.

I shrugged. "I'm sorry. I told you I would have to check my schedule, and I was booked solid today. Maybe next time you could call ahead."

Horace didn't seem to like that, and he raised his staff a little in my direction. Without thinking, I put a mental shield up, something my mother had taught me how to do a long time ago, for protection in case anyone tried to mentally harm me. At the time, I hadn't really understood why anyone would do that, but she had insisted that I study it anyway. And, I'm sad to say, this isn't the first time I've had to raise my shield.

I felt Horace's energy bounce off my mental shield and he winced slightly as I sent it back to him twofold, all while smiling brightly at him.

His eyes narrowed.

"Horace, have you heard about the murder last night?"

Luna and Miss Elva both sucked in a breath; I imagined they would've pummeled me if they could have.

"I have. Terrible tragedy," Horace said immediately. Screw this, I thought and reached out to scan his thoughts.

I was surprised when all I found was a black hole of nothingness. No thoughts, No emotions. No memories.

I'd never encountered such a thing before.

"It is. We're all praying for the poor man's family," Miss Elva said, effectively ending the conversation.

"Of course. We'll be sure to send a prayer to the gods and goddesses to protect his spirit and ask that it be given to the light," Horace said smoothly. He glanced up to see the setting sun sinking below the horizon, leaving only darkness.

"I must be starting the ceremony soon. Follow me."

I was fairly certain that was an order, and looked quickly at Luna for confirmation on what to do. She shrugged and nodded.

"I don't like that man," Rafe muttered in my ear as we followed Horace through the throngs of people emptying out of tents and funneling towards what looked like a huge pile of sticks.

"You and me both, Rafe."

Chapter Eighteen

"WHY CAN'T I question him about the murder?" I hissed to Miss Elva as we fell behind Horace, his horns visible among the crowd of people heading for the ritual space.

"Child, that man is not going to give you any information."

"Do you think he did it?"

"I think he's just about capable of anything. Horace is bat shit crazy."

"I tried to read his mind."

Miss Elva swung her head to look at me.

"What did you find?"

"Nothing. Not a thing. No memories, no thoughts. It was like a yawning abyss of nothingness."

"He blocked you," Luna said, overhearing our conversation.

"I blocked him," I corrected Luna.

"Blocked him from what?" she asked.

"He tried to send some sort of energy at me. Actually, I got the feeling he wanted to *take* from my energy. You know, like a psychic vampire? So I blocked him the way Mom taught me when I was younger. He knew it, too. I sent it back at him and he didn't like it."

Luna and Miss Elva stopped, giving each other looks before turning to me with matching postures, their hands on their hips.

"What?" I asked, genuinely confused.

"Child, you sure know a lot more magick than you are letting on about," Miss Elva said, clearly annoyed with me.

"No kidding. What the heck, Althea?" Luna asked, perturbed.

"I do?"

"Yeah, that's some higher level magick there. Blocking is one thing. Sending it back at him is another. I think Abigail and I need to have a talk," Luna said, speaking of my mother.

"I honestly didn't know I was doing magick. I thought that was just something you did to protect yourself from people stealing your power," I exclaimed. I was really beginning to get annoyed with everyone keeping me in the dark on things.

"Explain to me how she taught you," Miss Elva demanded.

"Right now?" We were nearing the edge of the circle, and I realized that huge pile of sticks was meant to be for a bonfire of sorts.

"I think we're going to need it," she said and I whipped my head around, watching as Horace began to circle the pile of sticks.

"You think he'll take your power?"

"I think he's going to try," Luna agreed.

"Don't you know any protection spells?"

"We do, but you already beat him at his own game. So I want to know what you did specifically," Luna said.

I thought back to what my mother had taught me when I was younger.

"It's kind of tricky, now that I think about it. Essentially it's like you have to let his power in for a brief second, almost as if you're tasting it, getting the flavor of it, you know? Then you counteract that particular flavor with whatever would be the power that would send it away – um, shoot, I'm not explaining this very well – like the opposite power," I said, stumbling over my words.

"So if his power is black licorice you would fight it with seafood," Luna mused.

"Or if his power was mud on the floor you'd use Mr. Clean," Miss Elva said.

"Yes! Like that. But you double up on it and kind of rubber-band it back, so it hits him twofold. You'll end up taking a ding out of his power while yours stays intact."

I really couldn't believe all the words that were coming out of my mouth. All those years spent listening at my mother's knee were starting to pay off.

"So Abigail must be magick," Luna mused, as we moved forward into the crowd.

"I think she and I need to have a conversation sometime soon," I agreed.

"Where is she now?"

"Probably Ireland. September," I mused and then paused. "Huh, maybe she is a witch if she always heads to Ireland for the September equinox."

Luna slapped her hand to her forehead and shook her

head at me. "I can't believe that I haven't picked up on this from her. Or that you haven't."

Okay, perhaps I'm not the most observant person. But it wasn't like my mom had *said* she was a witch. I just knew she was one of the best psychics in the world. The two are not synonymous.

Nor are they mutually exclusive.

Rolling that new thought around in my brain, I followed Luna and Miss Elva as we flowed with the crowd around to where Horace was pacing by the pile of sticks. Then two of his henchmen – can I call them that? I'm calling them that – used large torches to set the structure alight. It was all very primal, and as the flames licked along the wood, a sense of foreboding snuck over me.

"Guys, let's stay back behind everyone," I whispered as a hush fell over the crowd and drums began to beat in unison. It was a weird, pulsing, rhythmic beat and I began to feel the sound reverberate through me as voices took up a chant.

"Is this normal?" I hissed to Luna, and she turned and smiled at me.

"So far, yes. Drums and chanting are very much a part of Pagan rituals. So far, so good. It's Horace we need to keep an eye on."

So I kept my eyes on Horace as he began to address the crowd. As speakers went, he was fairly animated, and I could see the wave of charisma pouring off him as he spoke to his audience. It was easy to see why this man had cultivated so many followers of his radical offshoot to the traditional Pagan religion. I began to wonder where the "radical" part came in, because Luna seemed to think that most of what we'd seen today was status quo for a Pagan festival.

"And now, I'd like to bring forth three special guests."

I was jerked out of my thoughts and my mouth dropped open to see Horace with both his arms extended, welcoming us forward as the crowd parted around us. The fire danced behind him, illuminating the horns but keeping Horace's eyes in shadow as the chanting rose and people began to push us forward.

I'd just discovered the radical part.

Chapter Nineteen

THE CROWD SURGED EXCITEDLY around us, people chanting and cheering as we were pushed forward to where Horace stood. The cheers were good-natured and people seemed to be looking forward to the main ceremony of Mabon with excitement. I suspected we were the only ones with any sort of distrust towards Horace.

"I know you didn't just put your hand on my cloak," Miss Elva scolded an overzealous man wearing nothing but a white linen maxi skirt and a crown of laurel leaves.

He raised his hands. "It's all good," he said.

"It most certainly is not. These crystals are hand sewn," Miss Elva said, and with a glittery swirl of her cape, she left the man gaping behind her. I shrugged my shoulders helplessly at him as I passed.

You don't mess with Miss Elva's cloak.

Horace turned, his hands raised high in the air, to quiet the crowd. The drums continued, now with a softer rhythm, so when his voice rang out across the crowd, it seemed to hold an ominous undertone. The flames flickering behind him coupled with the light from the full moon created an eerie backdrop.

"Brothers and sisters, I want to provide a special welcome for our guests," Horace intoned, his horns bobbing wildly on his head as he shouted to the crowd. Alarm bells started ringing in my head and I saw Miss Elva's hand tighten into a fist.

"We are so lucky to have such esteemed guests with us today," Horace continued, a maniacal smile on his face, his eyes catching the light of the fire.

"Please welcome Luna, Tequila Key's own white witch; Althea, a psychic and sorceress; and the one and only – Miss Elva, the most famous voodoo priestess in all of Florida!"

My mouth went dry as our identities were outed and the crowd cheered in welcome.

Here's the thing: I don't hide the fact that I'm a psychic. I mean, I make my living from it. But Luna doesn't let on that she's a white witch to anyone except her fellow Wiccans and her closest friends. Chalk up another check mark in the naughty column for ol' Horace. He'd also clearly known who Miss Elva was and had pretended that he hadn't. My distrust for Horace grew.

Twice now I'd been referred to as a sorceress. While I appreciated the elevation of my humble title of psychic to something much more glamorous, I was going to have to have a talk with Luna when this was all over.

For now, I focused my attention back on Horace, my shoulders tensed as I waited for whatever would come next.

"Blessed be, my followers," Horace began, reaching

his arms high to the sky again as he began to hop gently from one foot to the other, each footfall in time with the beat of the drum.

I thought it was interesting that he called the Pagans his followers. From what I knew of the Pagan religion, festivals were put on collectively by a council each year and while there was a Master of Ceremonies of sorts, the group followed a religion, not a person. Which just goes to show the power of a charismatic, fanatical, and highly egotistical leader, I thought, almost rolling my eyes but catching myself because Horace was watching me.

"Tonight, we honor our Gods and Goddesses of above and of below, as in this moment, day and night are equal forces and darkness begins its ascendancy."

Luna whipped her head around to meet my eyes.

"I'm assuming this isn't normal?" I whispered.

"Not even close. He's going to summon the darkness. Protect yourself, now," Luna ordered and I saw Miss Elva nod in my direction.

I watched as Horace began to cast a circle, invoking the watchtowers I'd learned the other night on the beach. I noticed that he cast the circle smaller, around himself and the three of us, while the crowd of people remained outside of it.

"I think this is the part in the movies where we're supposed to run," I said to Miss Elva. She just shook her head at me, her eyes wide in her face.

"Don't break the circle, Althea. We're in this now."

Crap, I thought as I dug my toe into the dirt, wondering if my cell phone would work out here. I had stashed it in my bra, 'cause I'm smart like that. Okay, well, maybe not, but I was trying to be better about learning from past experiences.

"Be here, oh gods and goddesses of the darkness, and bless us with your presence," Horace intoned, his voice a low monotone. The beat of the drum picked up as he turned to the crowd and began to chant.

"Hoof and horn, hoof and horn,

All who die shall be reborn."

I shivered at the words and cast a glance at Luna.

"Not an atypical chant. It's meant to celebrate the cyclical nature of life, but I don't think that's how Horace is using it. He keeps calling the gods of the dark, which is not a Pagan practice."

"I will now draw down the moon," Horace called and the cheers rose. As the drumbeats intensified, I began to feel a pulsing energy pushing at me.

"What the hell does that mean?" I hissed to Miss Elva.

"It's usually a way to communicate with the goddess, but he's not going to do that. Ladies, protect yourselves. Immediately," Miss Elva said, stepping one foot in front of us and spreading her cloak wide with her hands.

Rafe buzzed around her head, worry etched across his face, as he trained his eyes on Horace.

"Althea, do the bubble of white light," Luna hissed and then closed her eyes; I could see her mouth moving as she chanted something to herself.

The bubble of white light Luna was referring to was an imagery she had taught me earlier this month; in fact, it was one of the first things she had taught me when she figured out I had some magick in me. Essentially, all I had to do was envision a ball of white light surrounding me, while asking my angels to protect me. I'd tried it a few times before and found it to be fairly easy.

My eyes flicked back to the chanting crowd. Guilt kicked up in my gut and I shook my head, hoping I wasn't going to open myself to harm by including them in my vision. But I couldn't just not protect them.

Closing my eyes for a moment, I centered myself and took a deep breath, then envisioned a circular donut of white light, a hole in the middle where the fire and Horace stood, coming down and enclosing myself, Luna, Miss Elva, Rafe, and the entire crowd in its warm glow of protection.

"Harm none," I began to chant, not knowing if what I was saying was correct, but the intention was pure. Opening my eyes, I saw Miss Elva and Luna looking at me, surprise painted across their faces.

I turned to watch Horace, trying to hold the donut of protection – so sue me, I like donuts – while he hopped ever more fervently from side to side, his horns bouncing back and forth, his chest thrust to the sky.

"Oh goddess of the moon, shine light into darkness, and enter me now as I pull all power to me. Come within, come within, come within!"

I gasped as I felt Horace fire a bolt of energy directly at me. It was much like what he'd done earlier, but tenfold the power this time. I finally realized what he was trying to do.

"He's trying to steal everyone's powers," I gasped, throwing my mental shield up as well as holding the protective donut strong. This was beyond ridiculous, I thought as a trickle of sweat snaked down my neck and beneath my dress.

"A psychic vampire," Miss Elva hissed.

"He's trying to steal our powers *and* summon powers from below. We'd better step back, now," Luna insisted, as Horace's eyes rolled back in his head and he began to speak in tongues, guttural snorts and spittle frothing from his mouth.

I found myself unable to look away as we pressed backwards into the crowd, allowing ourselves to be swallowed by the people. This time, the crowd murmured angrily amongst themselves and a low rumble of protest began as Horace continued to dance.

"What's happening?" I asked Miss Elva.

"He was supposed to draw down the moon. It's a ceremony used to contact one of the Goddesses. Instead he's trying to take the power of those in the circle and of a demon. His ego has gotten the better of him."

I gasped and whipped my head around. "Luna! We broke the circle!"

"It's okay, I've got us," Luna said, biting her bottom lip as sweat poured over her brow. I was momentarily distracted. Luna never sweats.

The earth began to tremble beneath our feet and I won't lie, I shrieked.

"Hold your protection," Miss Elva shouted and I focused.

"Harm none, harm none, harm none," I chanted, out loud this time, not caring who heard me.

The earth shook, like an honest to god earthquake, and

split. A flash of light, far brighter than any lightning, blinded us, causing the crowd to scream.

Silence fell over the entire assembly for a single second.

"Run," Luna shouted.

And run we did.

Chapter Twenty

IT'S NOT LIKE I'm totally out of shape, but by the time we got to the car, I kind of felt like I was going to throw up. I'm blaming it on the humidity.

"What the hell was that?" I shrieked, as Luna floored her Bug past the surprised man sitting at the registration table. Yes, that was twice in one day that I'd shrieked. Let's not dwell on it too much.

"That man is out of his damn mind," Miss Elva puffed from the front seat, waving her hands at her face to cool herself down. Luna hit the button for the air conditioner as we barreled down the gravel road away from the festival.

"Are you all right, my lovemountain?" Rafe asked and Miss Elva chuckled.

"I like having him around," she decided.

"He's all yours," I insisted and Miss Elva laughed again.

"Luna, what happened back there?" I asked, my breathing beginning to return to a slightly more normal pace, though my back was sticky with sweat.

"He tried to take our power. Pretty much like you said – a psychic vampire who feeds on power."

"But what about the summoning the dark underlords thing?" I asked, pushing my hair back from my face.

"I think he tried to cover what he was doing with a 'draw down the moon' ritual. Usually the ritual is considered quite holy and beautiful, a way to connect with the Goddess Diana or one of the other goddesses. I've been present for a few, and found them to be really lovely," Luna said, checking her rearview mirror.

"This was not lovely."

"No, what he was trying to do was take power. From us. From the crowd. And from those below," Miss Elva said ominously.

"Why would someone do that?"

"To feed their ego. The more power he has, the more he can control people. It's a dangerous game to play," Luna said as we approached the end of the gravel road where we would turn back towards civilization.

"Goddesses are gonna smack him down," Miss Elva observed.

"What do you mean by that?"

"Goddesses don't like when someone tries to trifle with that stuff. Just you watch, Horace is going to get what's coming to him."

"Did you curse him?" I asked. Miss Elva was legendary for coming up with the best and most inventive curses.

"Child, I didn't have to. That man cursed himself when he started trying to steal power from Goddesses. Trust me, he's in for it."

"I suppose that's something, then," I said, craning my neck to look behind us. "There aren't, like, demons or anything coming after us, are there?"

"Not us, child, not us," Miss Elva said.

"Speaking of no harm coming to us," Luna said, as we sped towards downtown Tequila Key, "what was that little magickal number you pulled back there?"

"Me? What about *you*? How come we could leave the circle and not be harmed? I was convinced we'd pick up another Rafe."

Rafe sniffed beside me, his nose in the air. "You'd only be so lucky."

"There is a little-known spell for breaking a circle when the one who cast it has ill intentions toward you. It's old magick," Luna said and Miss Elva nodded her head.

"That's a good one, Luna child. I hadn't even thought of that one."

"Well, thank you. I'm glad we didn't get zapped by whatever that light was," I said, running my hands up and down my arms to soothe myself.

"You should be proud of yourself, Thea. You sure did a good job of protecting a whole lot of people," Miss Elva said.

"I tried," I said, shrugging it away.

Luna glanced at me in the rearview mirror; I could just see her eyes in the glow of the console lights.

"Tell me how you controlled it like you did."

"I don't know, really. I thought of the white bubble and was starting the protection spell when I looked around at all the people behind me. I kind of felt guilty that I was just going to protect us and not everyone else, so I made a magickal donut."

Miss Elva snorted, and then began to rock back and forth in her seat, wheezing as she slapped her knee.

"A magickal donut?" Luna squeaked.

"Yeah, one that was basically a circular protective ring around us and everyone outside the circle, with a hole in the middle for whatever nonsense Horace was about to pull onto himself," I shrugged, feeling a little foolish.

"Only you would make a magickal donut," Luna said, shaking her head back and forth before she began to laugh.

"I like donuts," I protested.

"Who doesn't?" Miss Elva laughed.

Lights flashed across the interior of the car and I froze, fear racing up my spine.

"You've got to be kidding me," I groaned.

"Nope, we're totally getting pulled over," Luna swore and eased the car to the side of the road, the interior of the car silent as we waited for Chief Thomas to approach.

I swear – it was almost like it was a full moon or something.

Oh wait.

"Evening," Chief Thomas said as he leaned down to look in the car, the light from his flashlight blinding us momentarily before he lowered it. "Ladies."

"Chief Thomas," we all chorused dutifully, and he shook his head.

"Do you know why I'm pulling you over?" Chief Thomas asked Luna, his eyes serious.

"Because I was speeding?"

"Yes, you were. Going twelve over. You know you

can't drive like that in a small town like this. What's the hurry?"

"Miss Elva wants a donut," I piped up, and felt the seat in front of me shake as laughter rippled through Miss Elva.

Chief Thomas looked at me and a wisp of a smile crossed his face.

"Well now, I can certainly understand the pressing need for a donut once in a while," Chief Thomas agreed. "Y'all coming from that festival?"

"No, just coming from an early Halloween party down in Looe Key," I said. Wow, the lies were strong with me tonight.

"An early Halloween party?" Chief Thomas raised his eyebrow at me.

"She's lying," Luna sighed and shook her head, smiling sweetly at Chief Thomas. "We were at a private party giving readings. We always dress like this when we get hired out. You know, play into the stereotype a bit. It gets us more tips," Luna explained. I saw Chief Thomas's eyes skim down Luna's nude dress and he nodded.

"Makes sense."

"We really were just hungry. Hoping to get to Lucky's before they stop serving food," I added.

The walkie-talkie at Chief Thomas's waist squawked and he stepped back a pace, raising his finger. Listening, he responded. "On it." Then he approached the car once more.

"Ladies, go get that meal. I'll follow up if I have any issues." With that, he all but ran back to his car. I watched as he whipped a fast U-turn and sped back in the direction we had come.

"He's going to the festival."

"That he is. Non-magickal people will have reported that earthquake."

Luna pulled the car back out onto the highway.

"Are we really going to Lucky's?"

"Oh yeah. I can't wait until Beau gets a load of our outfits."

Chapter Twenty-One

"MY, MY, MY, what do we have here? Did I miss an invite? Is it Carnival up in here?" Beau called, his hands on his hips as he ran his eyes up and down our outfits.

"Careful, child, I'm not afraid to curse you into being a straight man," Miss Elva cautioned as she maneuvered herself onto a stool by the bar. Beau laughed, and leaned over to smack a kiss on her cheek.

"My worst nightmare." He shivered dramatically.

Lucky's was fairly slow for a Saturday night, but I wasn't surprised. Between the festival in town and a murderer on the loose, people were probably sticking pretty close to home. A few patrons lingered over their food at worn teak tables out on the verandah, the tiki torches flickering in the breeze as they dispelled the bugs.

"Is food done for the night?"

"Mostly. I'll give you our limited late-night menu though," Beau said, sliding a smaller menu towards us.

Frankly, I didn't care. Any sustenance would do. After what we'd seen tonight, I was ravenous.

A laugh that I knew well caused me to raise an eyebrow. Beau braced his hands on the bar top in front of me and leaned in.

"Play nice," he ordered.

"Why wouldn't I?" I smiled at him. We both knew I was lying. He just shook his head at me and pulled out his waiter's pad.

"Care to order?"

"Burger, you know what I like," I said, distracted by the fact that Trace was on a date out on the verandah. God, didn't he know this was my place? Beau was my best friend after all. Trace should know better than to bring his dates here. Feeling extraordinarily put out, I kept my eyes trained on the bar as I heard him approach.

"Hey, Trace," Luna finally said and I knew I had to turn or I would appear to be acting like a petulant child. Which I certainly wasn't, I thought as I pulled in my lower lip and turned around with a bright smile on my face.

"Hey, how's it going?" I asked, brightly.

Trace looked good. Like, *really* good. I hadn't seen him in a couple weeks, as we hadn't gone on our usual dive trips. Someone had been sleeping in more than usual, and I knew it had to do with the girl hanging on his arm. I included her in my smile, though mentally I was totally judging her.

"You guys remember Sienna, right?" Trace asked casually, his arm draped over her shoulders. Sienna smiled at us, though her eyes narrowed for a moment when her glance slid over me. I knew she was remembering when I'd been bitchy to her on Trace's boat a while back.

I had to admit they looked cute together. Trace's lanky

build, his lightweight plaid button-down rolled to his elbows to reveal his tattoos, and his sun-kissed hair pulled back at his neck paired nicely with her petite frame, sandy blonde hair, and perky-all-over cheerleader appeal. I could see why he'd gone for her.

I just didn't have to like it.

"Did you guys come from a costume party or something?" Sienna asked, wrinkling her nose at our outfits.

"Yup, massive one. You weren't invited?" I asked, raising an eyebrow at her. I saw the corner of Trace's mouth quirk slightly in a smile.

"No, but I'm new here, so I'm not surprised," Sienna said easily.

"Well, it was loads of fun. Maybe next time," I added, deciding not to be a total bitch. I didn't necessarily want to bully the poor girl for being new in town. It wasn't like she'd stolen my boyfriend, I silently reminded myself. I'm the one who had chosen Cash over Trace.

So why did it bother me so much to see Trace with another girl? I'd been friends with Trace for years now and we'd never crossed the line that would take us from friendship into something more. At least, not until a little while ago, when we'd both been single at the same time and Cash had entered the picture. All of a sudden, Trace had been all up in my personal space.

And I'd be lying if I said I hadn't liked it.

Let me tell you, it's no fun picking between two hot men. There's a good chance they'll both get fed up with you and kick you to the curb, and there's also a good chance you may pick the wrong one. I know it *sounds* like a fun problem to have, but the situation had bothered me more than I'd cared to admit at the time.

Now I was looking at Trace in a new light – and it had nothing to do with being dive buddies, and everything to do with being bedroom buddies. I blew out a breath and scolded myself. Clearly, Cash had been out of town for too long and my hormones were overtaking my usual good sense. Strike that – my occasional good sense.

It figures that two men would come along in my life at the exact same time. Or at least make their interest known at the exact same time. I mean, where'd they been the past six years when I'd been dating someone once every six months at best and supremely unhappy with my love life? Yes, I'd asked the universe for some help with my love life, and it had certainly delivered. A little too abundantly, I might add.

"Well, we're going to get going. We want to catch up on the last season of Scandal," Sienna chirped.

I raised my eyebrow at Trace and he blushed a little under my scrutiny, shrugging awkwardly.

"Have fun, see you tomorrow," I said pointedly to Trace.

"Yes, I can't wait to learn to dive," Sienna gushed and my eyes shot to Trace's face as I tilted my head in question. Did she just say she was joining us on our dive tomorrow?

Trace shrugged his shoulders guiltily.

"Yeah, um, I told Sienna I'd teach her the ropes. When she heard we were going diving in the morning, she told me how much she wanted to learn."

I glanced at Sienna and she met my look, her eyes wide and guileless.

Oh, I just *bet* you wanted to learn, I thought.

"Great! I'm sure she'll have fun seeing the sharks," I said breezily, turning back to the bar as my food was served, but not before I saw Sienna blanch a little.

"You didn't say anything about sharks," I heard her saying as Trace led her from the restaurant.

"Where does she think the sharks live?" I demanded of Luna.

"Maybe I'd better go along in the morning to make sure you don't drown her," Luna said, taking a bite of her salad.

"I promise not to drown her," I grumbled over the salty crispiness of my French fry. I couldn't believe Trace was bringing his new girlfriend on our dive. That was *our* time together. For years, Trace had been taking me out on his dive boat in the very early mornings, before he had customers on board for the day. I used the time to work on my underwater photography, and he used the time to just chill out underwater without having to be responsible for anyone else's safety. It was a win-win for us both, and I was more than a bit annoyed that Sienna would be joining us tomorrow.

"I don't know what your problem is anyway, Thea. You've got a scrumptious man, if I recall correctly?" Beau lectured me.

I shrugged one shoulder non-committedly, and he raised an eyebrow.

"I mean, I do. Yes. I think I do. We talk a lot."

"See, that's huge right there. Everyone knows guys

don't like to talk on the phone," Beau nodded at me as he slid a fresh mojito across the bar to me.

"Why can't you have them both? That's what I would do," Miss Elva said. I gaped at her.

"You can't have *both*," I argued.

"Says you. You can if you're Miss Elva," Miss Elva chortled, and I almost spit out my food laughing at the horrified look on Rafe's face.

"What are you looking at?" Beau asked, following my gaze. I realized I'd grown used to Rafe hanging around.

"My ghost boyfriend," Miss Elva said. "He's a little pissed that I'm talking about taking more than one lover at a time." She turned to lecture the ghost. "Now, Rafe, you're going to have to realize – you can't have me all to yourself until I'm in the spirit world with you."

Beau's mouth dropped open. Then he shook his head. "Of course, why *wouldn't* she be talking to her ghost boyfriend?" he asked.

"I kind of have a ghost boyfriend too," I muttered, and Luna shoved me a little in my chair.

"Whining is not very becoming. You're gonna feel bad about that when Cash comes back down here and rocks your world," Luna scolded gently.

"Probably. But for now, the only world that's getting rocked is Sienna's tomorrow," I promised.

"You leave that poor girl alone. We've got enough problems on our plate without you trying to take down some stick of a girl," Miss Elva lectured.

"What other problems?" Beau asked, reaching across the bar to pick up Miss Elva's empty glass. He held it up in question, and she waved her hand in a 'go ahead' gesture.

"Well, we've got a murder to solve, for one," Miss Elva began.

"Please tell me you aren't trying to solve that murder out on the beach," Beau gasped.

Luna and I looked at each other, guilt evident on our faces.

"What did you two do?" Beau demanded.

"Shhh," Luna hissed, and we leaned forward so that only Beau could hear us.

"We were on the beach the night of the murder. I was teaching Althea how to cast a circle. The dead body ended up smack dab on our circle," Luna whispered and Beau gasped, clutching his hand to his heart.

"Y'all are going to give me a heart attack. I can't even with you two. This is not good," Beau shook his head gravely.

"Thanks, Mr. Obvious," I said, glaring at him.

"Althea left her shoes there too. And whatever else she may have dropped when we ran."

"Why'd you run?" Miss Elva asked curiously. "Did my sweet Rafe scare you?"

Rafe puffed out his chest at her words, and I rolled my eyes.

"I just felt like there was an evil presence on the beach and my gut said to run," I said, shoving another French fry in my mouth. I was stress eating. Who cares?

"And now Thea thinks there's going to be another murder," Luna said quietly, causing Beau's eyes to go wide in his handsome face.

"No," he said.

"Yes, and I don't know when or how because *someone*

interrupted my vision today," I said, glaring at Rafe. He shrank to hide behind Miss Elva.

"You leave Rafe alone. He means well."

I hate when people say that. It's not necessarily a positive thing and I feel like it's kind of a cop-out – a way to excuse bad behavior. I gave Rafe the stink eye before returning to the conversation with Beau.

"Is that what you were doing tonight? Gathering clues?" Beau asked as he washed glasses. He paused to wave at a couple who were leaving.

"We were going to, but the festival took a turn for the worse," Luna said, and I continued to eat my meal, letting Luna fill Beau in on the night's events. By the time she finished, he was fanning his face with a dishtowel.

"Lawd, remind me to get off work more often. Y'all had yourselves some excitement tonight," Beau exclaimed.

"Trust me, it's not as much fun as it sounds."

It really wasn't. I hate thinking about a murderer lurking amongst us. It messes with what I really want to think about – which is Cash and when I'll see him next.

"So, all roads lead to this Horace character?" Beau asked.

"It certainly seems like that," Luna agreed, biting at her lower lip. I didn't say anything, and only looked up when the silence grew and I realized that everyone was looking at me.

"What?"

"Do you think Horace did this?" Beau asked, enunciating slowly as if I couldn't understand English. I picked an ice cube out of my drink and threw it at him.

"I don't know," I answered honestly, fidgeting with my

napkin. "It's like, yes, I do, because Horace is crazy and it's easy to hate him. But then there's a side of me that feels like this is too neatly wrapped up in a bow for us."

"You think it's a setup," Beau said.

I shrugged. "Could be. I don't know. I will say that, in my brief time around Horace, he's ordered me around and tried to steal power from me, both of which I do not like, so you pretty much know where he stands with me."

"So what now?" Beau asked.

"Tomorrow night we go back to the beach." I shrugged as Miss Elva and Luna both gaped at me. "What? We have nothing else to go on. Might as well get a feel for it," I said.

"Why not tonight?"

"I've reached my limit of crazy for the night. It's a full moon, and we've had enough shit go down. I want my pajamas, a glass of wine, Hank, and a good night's sleep before I drown Sienna in the morning."

"Girl, you'd better get your jealousy in check real quick. Sienna isn't going anywhere anytime soon, and you know it," Beau called.

Didn't I just.

Chapter Twenty-Two

AFTER A VERY DISGRUNTLED night of sleep – even Hank got annoyed with my tossing and turning and eventually hopped from my bed to go sleep on his own – I glared at my phone when it blared the alarm.

Cash hadn't called last night, which had annoyed me even more. I'd been studiously working on not being a clingy girlfriend, so I hadn't texted him either. Let him wonder just what I was up to.

Hank seemed to sense my crankiness, and he tilted his head at me as he pawed to get up on the bed.

"Sorry, buddy," I said, reaching down to pull him up onto the bed for a quick snuggle.

Nothing makes you feel better in the morning than sweet puppy snuggles. Feeling marginally better, I got up and took a quick rinse in the shower to clear my head, and shaved all the pertinent spots. The thought of Sienna in her neon bikini stopped my hand when I went to pull my usual dive swimsuit out of the drawer. Typically I wore a pretty skimpy swimsuit that fit easily under my skin wetsuit for diving. My hand hovered over my bikini as doubts flooded in about being directly compared to Sienna's svelte figure.

Annoyed with myself for feeling insecure, I grabbed my bikini anyway. Just because I had a few extra pounds on my body didn't mean I wasn't gorgeous. Wondering why I couldn't channel Miss Elva's confidence, I slipped the suit on and pulled a simple tank dress cover-up over it.

"Let's get you breakfast," I said to Hank and he snorted in agreement as he raced down the steps in front of me, his little body wriggling in joy for his most favorite part of the day.

"Sit," I ordered, standing above his bowl with a scoop of food in my hand. Hank sat obediently.

"Good boy. Now, moonwalk."

Hank crouched and then lifting one paw high, he began to move backwards slowly, alternating which paw he lifted high.

"Yes!" I shouted and Hank responded to my excitement with a howl as he whipped his little body in circles.

Okay, we might have been a little over-excited, but we'd been working on moonwalk for a while.

Upon further reflection, maybe it's better that I stay single, I thought as I poured myself a quick cup of coffee from the pot I'd set on timer the night before.

Sliding the back door open, I packed my dive bag as Hank did his business. I was still feeling somewhat cranky from lack of sleep, but I was also worried about what was going to happen next with the murderer. My thoughts flashed back to the scene at the festival last night. I wondered what had happened to Horace, and whether the crowd of people had kicked him out last night or if the crowd had welcomed him back into the fold?

My phone buzzed with an incoming text.

"I checked on Miss Elva. Nothing eventful through the night. Rafe stayed up and watched. I'm safe too. You?"

I loved Luna. She was so pragmatic, always thinking ahead.

"All good. Will text you after diving. You know. To let you know that I didn't kill Sienna."

"Please don't. I wanted to get a pedicure today, not deal with you and the cops."

"Fine, fine, fiiiiine." I texted back, laughing as I locked up my house and reached in the drawer for a squeaky toy for Hank.

"Ohh, a lobster today. Rock lobsta!" I sang, like the dork that I am, then threw the lobster across the room as I made my way out the front door.

Hopping on my beach cruiser, I pedaled my way through the streets, which were quiet this early in the morning. Deciding to cruise past Miss Elva's house, I turned on her street, biking slowly as I approached her house, enjoying the light breeze on my face.

I saw Rafe sitting on the front porch, almost as if he was waiting for me.

"Hey Rafe," I said quietly, looking around to make sure nobody else was on their front porches. I didn't want to look like a crazy person talking to myself.

"Miss Elva wanted me to wait for you," Rafe said by way of greeting.

"Oh great. What now, and where is *she*?"

"My queen needs her beauty sleep," Rafe explained.

"Go on," I gestured to Rafe.

"She wanted me to give you this," Rafe said, pointing at a small pouch that sat next to him on the railing. I immediately raised my hands and shook my head, as fear crept down my spine.

"Last time she had me carry a pouch, I got kidnapped."

"From what I understand, the pouch is what saved you," Rafe argued back.

Well, shit. The ghost had a point.

"I don't like this, Rafe," I said, leaving my bike and going up the railing to pick up the small leather pouch. I could feel the power humming from it and could only imagine what Miss Elva had put in it.

"She was up late working on this. She said wait until dark to use it. You'll know when," Rafe shrugged.

"This just made my day a whole lot worse," I grumbled, picking up the pouch and carefully putting it into the pocket of my dive bag.

"At least you have protection," Rafe pointed out.

"Yeah, but from what? That's what I'm worried about."

"Maybe from a shark," Rafe said, and I slid a glance at him as I got on my bike.

"Nice to see your sense of humor is intact," I said, waving goodbye as I continued on my way to the wharf.

A shark was the last thing I was worried about.

Chapter Twenty-Three

I COULDN'T HELP IT – I cringed when I walked down the floating dock, waving at the fishermen stocking their boats with bait, as I got to the end and saw Sienna kissing Trace.

Gauntlet thrown, Sienna, gauntlet thrown.

Now I was glad I'd worn my skimpy bikini. Let's show this stick of a girl what a real woman looks like, I thought uncharitably as I cleared my throat loudly before hopping onto Trace's dive boat.

"Oh, hey Althea," Sienna said sweetly, and I smiled brightly at her. I wondered what she would do if I walked over and wrapped my arms around Trace and pulled him in for a big kiss.

My thoughts must have shown on my face because Trace's eyes narrowed at the corners and he shook his head slightly at me.

"Hey, Sienna," I said, moving past her to put my bag on a bench at the back. Without really thinking about it, I began to go through our morning routine. I unpacked my bag and hooked my regulator up to my tank, threading the regulator hoses through my BCD. When Trace started the boat's engines, I walked to the front and hopped onto the dock, crouching to unravel the rope from where it wound around the hook on the dock. As Trace reversed slowly, I held the rope and walked towards the end of the dock, jumping easily back onto the boat at the last minute. Sienna watched all of this carefully, her eyes darting between Trace and me, and I knew she was assessing our established relationship patterns.

"Where are we going today?" I asked, stopping on my way from the front of the boat back towards where my stuff lay on a bench. Trace stood at the wheel, motoring us from the channel that would feed us out into the ocean.

"I was thinking just out to Shipwreck Reef," Trace said sheepishly and I tilted my head at him.

"If you're just going to take us to a snorkeling spot, I could've stayed home," I said, annoyed that I'd gotten up to go on a shallow water dive.

"But he said it would be a good spot for me to do my check-out dive," Sienna said, looking back and forth between us.

"You know I can't take her where we usually go. That's a little too advanced for her," Trace said, pleading with me to be nice.

"Just how often do you guys really go diving?" Sienna asked, her tone annoyed.

"Twice a week, usually," I said, smiling at her.

"Really? I didn't know that," Sienna said, her eyes on Trace. He just shrugged.

"It's nice to get out early before my day fills up with

clients. I like to have a little peace in the water," Trace explained.

"With her," Sienna asked pointedly.

"Yes, with me. I have thousands of dives under my belt and I'm also an accomplished underwater photographer. Trace doesn't have to worry about me in the water like he would with you," I said, not softening the sting in my words.

"Well, then I'll just have to catch up, won't I?" Sienna said, raising an eyebrow at me and standing her ground.

"You do that," I muttered as I finished checking my gear over and pulled my camera from its case. Shipwreck Reef was only a short ride away and I could already see the buoy marker bobbing in the water ahead of us. Pulling my dress over my head, I tucked it into my bag and walked to the front of the boat, not caring that both Sienna and Trace watched me in my little bikini.

The sun was already warm against my skin, even this early in the day. The wind was kicking up a bit from the west, and I wondered if we'd have any hurricanes coming our way this season. The large white ball of a buoy bobbed on shimmering aquamarine water, signaling that the reef was close and that the depth was shallow.

Oh well. Maybe I'd get some good macro shots while Trace dealt with Sienna.

I hooked the buoy line to the boat and then moved past Sienna, not caring that she was watching my every move. At this point, she should have been paying attention to how Trace was hooking up her gear instead of worrying about what I was doing. I slid into my skin wetsuit, pulling it all the way up and leaving the back loose.

"Can you zip me?" I asked sweetly, turning my back to Trace. Trace zipped me so quickly he almost caught my skin, and I shot a glare over my shoulder at him.

"I know this reef pretty well, so I'll just let you two do your thing."

Sitting down on the bench, I slid my arms into the BCD vest and worked my straps closed, watching as Sienna slid her neon-clad body into a wetsuit, smiling up at Trace as he zipped her.

Damn it. They were cute together.

But I would never do this again, I decided, standing hunched over from the weight of the tank on my back.

"Shit, Thea, let me help," Trace said, rushing to my side to assist with the heavy tank.

"It's fine," I said, crouching down until I sat at the loading platform. Trace stayed silent as he handed me my fins. Attaching both to my feet, I slid my mask over my face and tested my regulator, checking my dive computer one more time to make sure that I had full air.

"Ready?" Trace asked.

"Yup."

I stood with Trace's help and stepped to the edge of the platform. I could hear Trace lecturing Sienna behind me as I held my regulator and mask to my face with one hand, and my underwater camera in the other. I waited until the boat dipped low and then took a giant stride into the water, briefly going under the surface and then bobbing to the top, buoyant from the air I had filled my BCD vest with. Turning, I flashed Trace the OK sign.

"See, Sienna? That was a giant stride entry. And did you see how she immediately flashed me the okay sign?

You want to be in constant communication with your dive buddies."

I turned my head away from the boat, unable to watch Sienna running her hands up Trace's chest as he talked to her like she was a baby. Letting the air out of my BCD, I began my descent.

Into my happy place.

There's nothing quite like diving to take your mind off of anything going wrong in your world, I thought as I made it to the bottom fairly quickly. Checking my dive computer I saw that I was only at 43 feet of depth, and I rolled my eyes. Luckily, this reef was a healthy one so I adjusted my camera to set up for macro shots, knowing I'd have time to get up close and personal with some of the smaller marine lifeforms that hung out under ledges.

I was having some fun taking pictures of a grouper in a cleaning station under a ledge when I heard a scream tear through the water.

Whipping around, I saw Trace forcibly holding the regulator to Sienna's mouth as she screamed into it, bubbles all but free flowing around her head. Her body jerked back and forth as she flailed her arms, pointing off in the distance as Trace tried to calm her down.

Rolling onto my back, I looked to see what the fuss was about.

I was rewarded with the sight of a black-tipped reef shark in the distance, and I almost choked with laughter. The more Sienna struggled and flailed about in the water, the more she was going to look like a distressed fish. And you know what sharks like to eat?

Injured fish.

Smiling to myself, I kicked closer to the shark, adjusting my settings on my camera for a wide-angle shot. Holding the camera up, I took picture after picture as the shark swerved its way closer, curious to see what all the fuss was about.

I almost doubled over in laughter when Sienna's fin caught Trace between the legs and I saw him reach to cup himself. He grabbed between his legs and I could see his eyes wincing in pain behind his mask.

I bet he wished he'd dived with just me this morning, I thought, smiling at him with my eyes as he pulled Sienna back to the boat, forcing her to hover for a safety stop while she kicked in panicked circles.

The shark soon grew bored and moseyed off, and I saluted it silently for giving me one of the best laughs I'd had in a long time.

Chapter Twenty-Four

ON THE WAY BACK IN, Sienna shot me dirty looks while she swallowed down the residual sobs that still shuddered through her.

"You know, reef sharks aren't all that dangerous," I offered, unwrapping a granola bar as the boat bounced through the waves.

"It's a *shark*. You promised there wouldn't be sharks," Sienna shot a glare at Trace, her towel wrapped tightly around her shoulders.

"Well, Sienna, he really can't control that. It's the ocean. That's where the sharks live. As well as the whales, the stingrays, and the moray eels. I mean, that's their home. What were you expecting when you went in the ocean?"

"I don't know. I just thought I'd see a turtle or like a clown fish, like Nemo," Sienna said, swiping a fist across her eyes.

"Clown fish aren't even found here…" I trailed off as

Trace shook his head at me. He didn't want me to talk sense into her? Fine, he could deal with it himself then.

I busied myself with rinsing my camera equipment in the freshwater bin, secretly hoping I'd gotten the shot of Sienna nailing Trace with her fin between his legs. That one might be a framer, I thought with a wicked smile as I packed up and unhooked my regulators.

"Looks like we've got company," Trace said grumpily as he slowed the boat's approach to the dock. My head snapped up at his tone and I turned, shading my eyes as I saw who was standing waiting for me at the dock.

"Cash!" I might have squealed a bit.

Trace shot a disgusted glance at me.

"That guy."

Chapter Twenty-Five

ALL MY NASTY thoughts about Trace and Sienna left my head as I drank in the sight of Cash standing next to another man on the dock. He looked good, like someone I wanted to climb all over, but I reined my libido in as I waved at him.

Cash waved back, his teeth flashing white against his tan skin, his dark hair cropped close to his head. Though aviators shielded his eyes from the sun, I knew them to be a crystal-clear grey. At over six feet tall and with enough muscles to make any red-blooded woman drool, he all but turned me to putty when he was around.

I grinned at him foolishly as I waited for Trace to dock the boat, tossing Cash the line so he could tie us up.

"Who's that?" Sienna asked.

"My boyfriend," I said, watching as her eyes widened a bit as she swept her eyes over Cash.

I mean, it wasn't like Trace wasn't something to look at either. But just because you're on a diet doesn't mean you can't look at the menu, right?

I hopped off the boat, stumbling a bit as the dock dipped when I landed. Cash caught me.

"Hey," I said, grinning a little too widely as I looked up at him. Sure, I probably looked a mess with my hair wild from the salt water and mask marks on my face, but I didn't care. I was just happy to have Cash in front of me.

"Hey yourself," he said, before dipping his head and sliding a kiss across my lips. He tasted good, like sunshine and sin, and I leaned into him for just a moment, his very essence threatening to pull me under.

"Geez, guys, get a room," Trace called, pulling me from my moment.

Really, Trace?

I turned and shot him a glare, one hand on my hip. I'd refrained from saying anything when Sienna had been practically crawling all over him all day, and he's going to interrupt my one hello kiss? Please.

I opened my mouth to say something, but Cash pulled me back to him, brushing another kiss across my lips while he pulled me closer into his body before raising his head to look at Trace.

"Nice to see you as always, Trace," Cash called, the warm timbre of his voice echoing against my ear pressed to his chest. There was something about Cash that made me feel all dainty and feminine, when actually I was far from being either of those things.

Trace just nodded at him before turning to Sienna. I pulled back and smiled stupidly up at Cash.

"I wasn't expecting you so early," I gushed, not wanting to sound like I was gushing, but unable to conceal how excited I was to see him.

"Surprise," Cash said softly, his lips quirking in a smile just for me, making my insides feel like jelly.

"Ahem." The man behind him cleared his throat and Cash laughed, pulling back from me.

"Althea, I'd like you meet my brother, Dylan."

Well, color me surprised. Had I known I'd be meeting family today, I would have looked a little more presentable. Immediately reaching up to smooth my hair and praying I didn't have any boogers in my nose, I peeked around Cash to the man who stood behind him.

It was easy to see, now that we were close up, that Cash and Dylan were brothers. They were both close in height, with the same muscular build, though Dylan's hair was several shades lighter than Cash's. Black Wayfarer sunglasses concealed his eyes, and he wore a distressed grey t-shirt tucked into fitted seersucker shorts. He had an easy style about him, but it only took a quick brush of my power against his mind to know that this was the gay brother Cash had promised to introduce to Beau. Knowing Beau, he was going to faint on sight when he got an eyeful of Dylan.

"Hi Dylan, so nice to meet you. I'm sorry I'm kind of a mess, I've just been scuba diving," I explained, stepping around Cash and reaching out to shake Dylan's hand.

Dylan shook my hand and then, when most people would have let it go, he held it for a moment longer, openly perusing me. From anyone else it would have been rude, but I didn't get that sense from Dylan. After a moment, he turned to Cash and nodded.

"I like her," Dylan said. Cash laughed and ran a hand through his hair, causing a few short pieces to stick up and making me want to go over and smooth them down. Or run *my* hands through his hair. Or over his body.

Down, girl, I ordered myself.

"I like him as well," I told Cash, and he laughed again. "Wait – Dylan and Cash. Is there a theme here?"

"Our mom's a big music buff," Dylan laughed.

"Ahh, that makes sense," I said with a smile.

"We wanted to catch you early. I was hoping we could maybe poke around and look at few potential neighborhoods before going to lunch at Lucky's," Cash raised his eyebrow meaningfully at me. "Then maybe after, I can ditch this tagalong and you and I can have some alone time."

My mouth went dry at the thought.

"He means he wants to get in your pants," Dylan elaborated and I coughed, almost choking on a laugh.

"Thank you for the clarification, much appreciated," I choked, torn between hilarity and embarrassment.

"I think Beau's going to like him," I finally said, turning to look at Cash.

"Oh yeah, Dylan's going to owe me big time for this introduction," Cash agreed.

"Yes, I've heard many things about this Beau of yours. I can't wait to meet him," Dylan said with a smile.

"I'm sorry to interrupt, but Ms. Rose, we need to speak with you," said a voice from behind me and chills went down my spine.

I turned to see Chief Thomas and a deputy standing there.

"Hey now, what's going on here?" Cash asked, immediately stepping in front of me. Cash was naturally suspicious of the local law enforcement after my last run-in with the police.

My protector.

"Ms. Rose is a person of interest in an ongoing murder investigation. I'll need to speak with her now." Chief Thomas didn't even crack a smile, and that's when I knew things were about to get serious.

"Did something happen, Chief Thomas?" I asked, my spidey-senses tingling.

"Another body was discovered this morning."

I gasped. "Who is it? Please don't tell me it's someone I know."

"An investor in the condo development. Herman Lavish. Do you know him?"

Bewildered, I shook my head, but out of the corner of my eye, I saw Cash's shoulders tense.

"I knew him."

"Mr. Williams, we may need to talk to you as well. For now, we'll be taking Ms. Rose with us."

"Wait a minute, am I under arrest? Or are you *asking* to speak with me?"

Chief Thomas leveled a look at me, his shoulders back and his demeanor calm.

"I'm suggesting you come with me so that I may speak with you."

"Fine, let me get my stuff," I said, my cheeks flaming in embarrassment. The first time I meet a member of Cash's family, and here I am being called in by the local police force as a person of interest in a murder case. As first impressions went, it was pretty shitty.

I didn't even spare a glance for Sienna as I gathered

my dive bag, but Trace touched my shoulder as I passed him.

"Promise to call me? I'll be on standby," he whispered.

"Yeah, I will," I nodded dully, horrified that this was even going to become a thing.

All I could think about were my black flip-flops, forgotten on the beach where a murder had occurred.

Chapter Twenty-Six

A FEW OF the other dive boat crews, already back from their morning dives, looked at me curiously as I followed Chief Thomas down the dock, his deputy behind me. I know how it looked – like they were arresting me. I groaned as I thought about how quickly this gossip would fly around town.

Cash and Dylan fell in line behind us, and I kept my back straight, trying not to think about what Dylan would be telling Cash's family about me. Maybe I'd been silly to think that Cash and I would be a good fit. Perhaps he and I were just two different breeds. I couldn't imagine his mother being happy about her son dating a girl with tattoos who got hauled in for questioning by the cops.

I tried to shake off my negative thoughts as we drew near to where my bike was locked up.

"Chief Thomas, that's my bike. Should I follow you to the station?"

"Why don't you just ride with us? We'll give you a

ride back to your bike," Chief Thomas said lightly, and I stopped to square off with him.

"Listen, this is starting to sound eerily like I am being arrested. I'm psychic, remember? Don't try to pull shit over on me," I seethed and then clamped my lips together, looking briefly at the cloudless sky as I counted to five and mentally kicked myself.

I had no idea if Cash had told his family what I did for a living, but the cat was out of the bag on that one now, too. Chalk this up to one of the crappiest mornings ever.

"A psychic, huh?" I heard Dylan say to Cash as Chief Thomas held open the back door of his sheriff's car for me, confirming my suspicions that Cash hadn't told his brother what I did for a living. For some reason, this irked me even more and I found myself wanting to kick the back of the seat as Chief Thomas and his deputy got in front.

"Was this really necessary? You know I would have come down to the station," I pointed out as we drove through town.

"We'll take you back to your bike," Chief Thomas said calmly.

"That's not the point. That was the first time I was meeting one of Cash's family members. How do you think this is going to look?"

Chief Thomas shot me a brief look of sympathy over his shoulder as we pulled into the parking lot of the station.

"I'm sorry. Sometimes a murder investigation takes precedence over everyday life," Chief Thomas said, reminding me that sometimes it's not all about me.

I bit back my response as I followed Chief Thomas into the small station, my head hanging down.

Tequila Key doesn't have a lot of crime, and the police station reflected that. A small stucco building, it housed a two-person jail cell, a few offices, a front desk and waiting area, and an interrogation area, all painted in a cheerful, blinding turquoise. I have no idea why so many seaside businesses insist on painting the interior of their spaces the same color as the ocean, but there you have it.

I stiffened when I realized I was being led into the interrogation area.

"Now, why does it suddenly feel like I need to call my lawyer?" I asked lightly, standing on one side of a grey metal table while Chief Thomas took a seat across from me.

"Althea, you are not under arrest. This is an informal questioning. We could do this in my office as well; it's just that there are more chairs here," Chief Thomas sighed.

"But it's just me and you," I pointed out, still refusing to sit.

"Not for long it won't be," Chief Thomas grumbled and I looked up as I heard voices outside the door.

"Let him in," Chief Thomas called, and in a moment, Cash's strong frame filled the door.

Cash looked directly at me.

"Do you need a lawyer?"

My heart clenched a bit. He didn't even ask if I'd done anything wrong, he was just immediately ready to ride to my rescue. Oh yeah, I could see myself falling for this one, I thought.

"No, because I haven't done anything wrong," I said.

Cash moved around the side of the table and, taking

my hand, pulled me over next to him to sit in one of the two uncomfortable plastic chairs.

"Where's Dylan?"

"Getting coffee."

I nodded, biting my lip, unsure of how to proceed, so I allowed the silence to fill the room as Chief Thomas sighed and leaned back in his chair.

"Althea, you know that withholding information on a crime is illegal, right? It's technically blocking a police investigation."

Cash shot me a glance, but I just nodded, waiting to see what Chief Thomas had to say.

"We've had a report that you were on the beach the other night, along with Ms. Lavelle. Her car was seen leaving the beach."

Ice shot through my veins as I flashed back to our run from the beach and my forgotten flip-flops.

"Who told you that?" I asked, going on the defensive.

"It was an anonymous tip," Chief Thomas said. A muscle jumped in his cheek and I knew he was lying. Feeling no shame, I reached out and scanned his mind.

"Prudie?" I screeched, almost jumping out of my chair. Chief Thomas sighed and ran his hands over his face, shaking his head slightly.

"I keep forgetting you're psychic."

"How could you forget? I literally just brought it up moments ago, at the wharf," I pointed out, internally seething about that nasty gossip Prudie. I was already planning what I would do to ruin her life.

"Listen, it's been a long morning," Chief Thomas began, and I really looked at his face for the first time.

Dark smudges hung under his puffy eyes and I realized that he'd been up for a long time already this morning. Deciding to cut him some slack, since he had so recently helped rescue me from being held captive, I took pity on him.

"Sorry, but what the hell has that old bat been feeding you?"

"She reported seeing Luna's car driving away from that beach. Since it's an undeveloped area, not a lot of cars go down that road. I'm sorry, but I have to follow up every lead."

"How do you know *I* was in the car?" I asked.

"She said there were two people. You and Luna are always together; it was just a hunch," Chief Thomas sighed.

"Why am I here and Luna isn't, then?" I asked, pointedly.

The Chief hesitated. "I can't find her," he admitted and I felt my stomach drop.

"What do you mean you can't find her?" I asked, enunciating each word precisely as alarm bells went off in my head.

"Nobody is answering at her condo. Her car's there. Your store is locked. Nobody has seen her. She's not answering her phone."

"Did you knock on her door for a long time? Sometimes she sleeps in."

Chief Thomas leveled a look at me and I shrugged.

"Okay, okay. You knocked for a long time. I don't like this," I said, biting my lip. "Do you mind if I try to text her?"

"Go ahead," Chief Thomas said and I dug in my bag.

Hey, it's Thea. Text me immediately.

Then, feeling even more suspicious, I called her; the call went straight to voicemail.

"Now that's even more strange," I admitted, fear creeping up my spine.

"What?" Cash asked.

"Her phone never goes to voicemail. Never. She keeps it on in case her grandmother out at Seashores Living needs her. It's never, ever, off."

"I think it's time to tell me what's going on," Chief Thomas said gently.

I turned to see Cash watching me carefully, his eyes curious, but I read no judgment coming from him. Still, I wasn't entirely sure I wanted to tell him I'd been doing a magickal ritual naked on the beach with my white-witch best friend.

See, there's this point in new relationships where your significant other finds out who you really are. You know what I'm talking about – whether it's your secret addiction to the Bachelorette, your love of all things Disney, or that you close your eyes every time you go over a bridge – there's always this turning point where they pull that exterior flap away and take a peek at what's really going on inside. And it can be terrifying.

I wanted the high to last a little longer with Cash. I just didn't have faith that he would stick around once he really knew how weird my world was. I'm not apologizing for who I am – I'm just saying that I'm a realist. Not a lot of guys are going to stick around psychics and witches, and that's just a fact.

Could I hide it just a little bit longer? If I asked Cash to leave now, he'd be even more curious about what was going on, and I'd probably hurt his feelings as well. Not seeing a way out of this, I sighed and turned to Chief Thomas.

"We were at the beach that night," I said softly, looking down at the table.

"Jesus, Althea," Chief Thomas swore.

"I think you'd better catch me up on what's going on here," Cash said evenly, his eyes darting between Chief Thomas and me, his shoulders tense.

"Friday morning we discovered a body laid out on a pentagram on North Beach, where the new condo development is going in. Someone killed him, drilled holes in his head, then planted seeds and saplings in the holes."

"Saplings?" Cash said in confusion.

"Saplings. It looked like some sort of offering. There's a Pagan festival in town, so the manner of death could fall in line with some sort of weird offering to the earth. Then we found a second body this morning," Chief Thomas continued, rubbing his temples with his fingers. I felt kind of bad for him. Police work can be a thankless job sometimes.

"How was he murdered?" I asked softly, and Chief Thomas trained his eyes on me.

"This body was found where the hole for the foundation of the building has been dug. A chain had been wrapped around his neck and used to choke him."

I shivered at the thought of it, shaking my head in confusion.

"I don't understand. This is nothing like the other

murder. I'd thought it was Horace," I said, then trailed off as Chief Thomas raised an eyebrow at me.

"Who's Horace?"

I sighed, knowing I would have to backtrack now and go over the whole story. I didn't want to even start with it all as I was really worried about where Luna was.

"Were you at that beach last night?" Cash interrupted as I was about to speak.

"No, we weren't," I insisted, shaking my head back and forth fervently.

"No, that's right – you were coming from the other direction, very fast, now that I think about it," Chief Thomas said, rubbing his hand along his chin.

"Luna got pulled over after we left the Pagan festival last night," I said to Cash.

"Festival? I thought you said you were coming from a party, Ms. Rose. It seems like it's one lie after another with you," Chief Thomas said, anger making his cheeks flush red.

"Okay, here's the truth," I began, refusing to look at Cash.

Knowing I was about to lose him.

Chapter Twenty-Seven

"SO YOU'RE TELLING me you were learning a magickal ritual, is that correct?" Chief Thomas asked again. I shrugged, refusing to meet Cash's eyes, but I could feel how tense he was next to me.

"Not like, a bad one, or anything," I began.

"But there was a pentagram," Cash said, his voice angry.

"Not a *bad* pentagram," I insisted, turning to him.

"I don't know what a bad one is," Cash said, his lips thin with anger.

"Hey, I don't really know either. That's more Luna's territory. I just know that if it's facing up, or North, it's a good one," I explained helplessly.

"Okay, so what is the purpose of a good pentagram?" Chief Thomas asked gently.

"I honestly don't know. I probably should, but I don't. Basically Luna was teaching me the correct manner to cast a protective circle."

"And why would someone need to cast a protective

circle?" Chief Thomas said, as Cash swore and shook his head.

"Um, if you were going to run a ritual. You know, like setting a good intention, or seeking balance, bountiful harvest," I was blathering at this point, so concerned with Cash's dismissal of me that I didn't really know what I was saying.

"So... a dead body with saplings in his head could be a good gift for a bountiful harvest?" Chief Thomas asked slowly.

"God no, that's horrible. You don't offer gifts. At least not that I've learned. You just protect yourself and run the ritual. I'm sorry, I wish I knew more."

"So what would the purpose of a body on the pentagram be?" Chief Thomas asked.

"I don't know. I honestly think it was probably just happenstance. Like, it was already there, so they used it. I felt the evil; that's why we ran," I blurted, and Chief Thomas's mouth dropped open.

"You felt the evil? Is that so?" Cash said, turning to shoot a glare at me. "You know, you could have told me about some of this. This is quite a surprise for a Sunday morning."

"Well, if you had called me yesterday, I would have," I said indignantly.

"I was working. You know? Work? I don't have a set schedule like you do," Cash said hotly. "I was trying to finish things up so I could come down here and surprise my girlfriend, who is apparently running around on beaches with murderers and casting magick spells while I'm gone." His voice had risen to a shout and both Chief

Thomas and I sat back as silence – except for Cash taking a few deep breaths of air –filled the room.

See? This is why relationships suck. You have to tell your person what you're doing all the time. I hadn't talked to Cash since Friday, and all of a sudden he thought I was keeping a world of secrets from him. Completely annoyed, I hunched in my seat, turning my shoulder on him.

"Oh sure, go ahead. Be mad at me," Cash said, waving his hand in the air, a disgruntled look on his face.

"If we could focus?" Chief Thomas said, raising an eyebrow as he pursed his lips.

"Listen, we were done with the magick lesson and, well, you know, I have extra senses," I said, pointing to my head, and Chief Thomas nodded for me to continue. "So, I felt this, like, wave of evil press against us. It sort of rolled across the beach. And I just told Luna to run. So we ran. I forgot my shoes and everything, my feet got all cut up on the gravel."

I slid my right foot from my flip-flop and lifted it to show Chief Thomas the bottom, where I had a few cuts from the gravel. He nodded and gestured for me to put my foot back under the table.

"And the next thing I know, Prudie's in the coffee shop the next morning telling the whole town that a murdered body had been found where we'd been practicing magick the night before."

Chief Thomas sighed and pinched the bridge of his nose, clearly frustrated with me.

"Why didn't you tell me any of this?"

"I don't know," I replied honestly. "My last relationship with the town cop didn't end so well, if you remember. I think that's broken my trust of law enforcement."

"Althea, I'm on your side. I was on your side *last* time you guys found a dead body, if you'll remember."

"I know. I get that. I do like you and I know you're an honorable man," I admitted.

"Then you can't withhold information from me like this. You could have seen something that would help us," Chief Thomas explained. I blew out a long breath, leaning back in my chair and looking up at the ceiling for a moment, surprised to find I was dangerously close to tears.

"So you believe me?"

"Yes, I believe you. But I still want to know who this Horace guy is and what you were really doing last night," Chief Thomas said sternly.

"Yes, I'm dying to hear more," Cash said dryly, and I shot him a look.

"We went to that Pagan festival last night," I began, and Chief Thomas sighed.

"Why wouldn't you just say that when you got pulled over?" he asked.

"Yes, Thea. Why would you lie?" Cash asked. I swung on him.

"You know, you've got a lot of nerve coming in here and acting like this," I began, feeling my temper kick up.

"Would it kill you to just be honest? What am I supposed to think about this?" Cash asked.

"I haven't been dishonest," I pointed out. "This happened last night. We haven't really spoken yet. Stop acting like I've lied to you. It's not like I'm hunting you down asking you to account for every second you're not with me. You're being totally unfair," I seethed.

Cash looked suitably taken aback and he nodded once, briefly.

"I'm sorry. You're right," he said simply and I felt my temper ease a bit.

Great, Cash was a guy who apologized easily when he was wrong, too? He was a way better man than I deserved. As far as I'm concerned, I'm always right and my apologies come few and far between.

"Can we stay on track here?" Chief Thomas asked, checking his watch. He was right; I wanted to get out of here and find Luna. Her non-responsiveness was making me nervous.

"Horace is the leader of the radical Pagan group that's in town. He's into super weird shit. The reason we were speeding last night is that, when we were there for what should have been a celebratory full moon ritual, he started calling on evil spirits or something, and things got weird."

It was like I had sucked all the air out of the room as both men sat perfectly still, devouring my words.

"Define weird," Chief Thomas said.

"Like *weird*. Flash of light. Ground moving. People screaming. We ran for it," I said.

"That would explain the call I got about an earthquake," Chief Thomas mused, leaning back in his chair.

"Did you go to the festival to investigate?"

"Too many cars were leaving for me to get down the lane right away. By the time I got there, everything looked fairly normal. Mostly empty, and – well, as normal as one could expect for that type of gathering."

"Did you see a man in a loincloth with ram horns on his head?"

Cash just shook his head next to me, closing his eyes briefly.

"That I did not."

"That's your man. He kind of looks like Gandalf. You know, long flowing grey hair, thin, eyes that pierce through to your soul," I explained.

"I will take that under consideration," Chief Thomas said evenly.

"Listen, am I free to go here? I really want to find Luna. I'm starting to get worried," I admitted.

"Yes, you can go. But, and I'm asking you this very nicely, please keep me informed today. We've got a killer on the loose and I could use all the help I can get," Chief Thomas said, holding my gaze.

I appreciated that he was letting me go and that he was being honest with me. For that, I would return the favor.

"If I know anything, you'll know it," I agreed, getting out of my chair.

See? I know how to work well with others... when I feel like it.

Chapter Twenty-Eight

"WHY DOES IT seem like every time I'm around you, you're in some kind of trouble?" Cash mused as we made our way to his Jeep. He'd agreed to drive me back to my bike and I figured we might as well hash things out between us now.

Why bother putting off the inevitable?

"Listen, I get if this is too much for you. I know I'm probably not someone you'll want to introduce to your family. And, yeah, I don't lead a normal life. There's always going to be something you would consider abnormal going on with me," I shrugged my shoulders as I bit my lip and stared out the car window at the water. "And I don't want to be normal. I've never aspired to have the picket fence kind of life. If that's the type of girl you're looking for, well, we should probably just stop this in its tracks right now," I said, stiffly. There, I'd been an adult about it; no harm, no foul.

I gasped as Cash swerved suddenly to the side of the

road and all but pulled me into his lap as he crushed his lips to mine, taking me under his spell with all his heat and yearning. I could feel how much he wanted me, the desire pulsing off of him in waves, along with a layer of anger underneath. Not caring, I kissed him back, throwing myself into it. If this was to be our last kiss then I was going to get my money's worth.

Moments later, we broke apart, gasping for breath, and met each other's eyes.

"Stop trying to break up with me," Cash panted.

"Stop making me feel like you don't want to be with someone like me," I panted right back.

"Stop making assumptions about the type of girl I want to be with," Cash retorted, and I sat back, crossing my arms over my chest.

"Am I wrong?"

"You're so wrong," Cash muttered, pulling the car back out into traffic and proceeding to the wharf.

I bit back a smile as I felt warmth fill me. Okay, so maybe the day wasn't a total loss.

"The magick stuff doesn't freak you out?"

"We're going to have a nice long talk about all of that. But I think we need to find Luna first. And solve a murder, it seems," Cash said, getting out of the car and walking to my bike. I walked over to where he stood waiting.

"So, I'll see you later?" I asked, not sure what to do now.

"Give me the key to your bike chain. I'm going to throw your bike in the car and we are going to find Luna together. Like couples do," Cash said patiently and I couldn't help but grin at him a little stupidly.

So we were a couple after all. Apparently, it only took a morning at the police station to confirm that.

See? Definitely not your average girlfriend.

Chapter Twenty-Nine

WE STOPPED BY my house so I didn't have to spend all day in my bikini and cover-up. Hank was delighted to see Cash again, and I smiled as he raced in circles around Cash, dropping as many toys as he could find at Cash's feet.

"I'll let Hank out. You go change," Cash ordered.

I took my phone with me upstairs, continuing to glance at it every few seconds, hoping for a response from Luna. Hopping in the shower for a quick rinse, I tried to calm the beginning tendrils of panic that licked at my stomach and thought about what to do.

"As much as I'd like to join you in there, we should probably get moving," Cash called through the door, knocking lightly as it was slightly open.

"You could join me," I offered hopefully, panic quickly being replaced with lust.

"Oh, I'll join you later. And all night. And tomorrow morning too," Cash promised, as he opened the shower door to hand me a cup of coffee. I met his eyes with my mouth hanging open.

"I look forward to it," I said, gulping hot coffee and stinging my mouth as he left the bathroom chuckling.

Damn, that man was distracting.

Considering my wardrobe after my shower, I thought again of Cash's brother and pulled out my newest maxi dress, a white ombre dress that faded from white at the shoulders down to a deep sea blue at the bottom. It was cool, chic, and I was probably going to spill something on it by the end of the day since I don't do so well with white. But at least I was trying.

Taking a moment to run some gel through my curls, I stopped at my bathroom mirror to add some mascara and eyeliner, grabbed some dangly silver earrings from a dish, and chugged down the rest of my coffee. This was as good as it was going to get.

I snagged my phone from the counter and texted Miss Elva on the way down the stairs about Luna being missing in action. I hoped that maybe she would have a finding spell or would know something we could do to track her down.

"You look nice," Cash said from where he sat on a couch, Hank lying belly-up next to him. Hank was snorting gently as Cash scratched his stomach and there was an expression of pure bliss on his face.

"Hank loves having his belly scratched," I pointed out, moving across the room to drop onto the couch next to him.

"He's pretty dang cute, farts and all," Cash admitted and I laughed, remembering the time Hank's particular brand of noxious gas had ended a makeout session for Cash and me.

My phone dinged with a text and I felt my heart flutter as I grabbed it.

"Luna?" Cash asked, leaning forward.

"Miss Elva," I said, shaking my head. "She wants to come help look for Luna. Chief Thomas must have contacted her."

"I haven't met this Miss Elva yet," Cash said and I raised an eyebrow at him, trying to decide if I wanted to give him any warning or let the full force of all that is Miss Elva hit him.

Deciding he'd already had enough shocks for the day, I patted his knee before standing.

"How do you feel about voodoo priestesses?"

Cash paused halfway off the couch and looked at me.

"I've never had to actually consider that question before," he admitted.

"See? Isn't it fun dating me?"

"I suspect there will never be a dull moment," Cash agreed.

Chapter Thirty

"STAY HERE, I'LL go get her," I instructed him and hopped out. Climbing the porch stairs quickly, I knocked on the weathered door and waited until I heard Miss Elva call for me to come in.

"Hey, Miss Elva," I called, stepping into her house.

Okay, so maybe I'm downplaying that a little a bit. Stepping from Miss Elva's porch into her house is like stepping from everyday life into an Alice in Wonderland room.

There is just so much *stuff.* Everywhere. It's like stimulation overload with no rhyme or reason to it. It's not like it's a hoarder's paradise or anything like that; it's just that every available space is filled with something. Next to a sofa straight out of a Restoration Hardware catalog was an old medicine cabinet hanging on the wall, its shelves crammed with bottles full of who-knows-what and animal skulls. Other shelves held prayer candles to every saint you could imagine. It didn't matter where you looked, there would be something intriguing there to grab your interest.

One of these days I was going to actually come hang out at Miss Elva's and have her tell me the stories behind the goods that cluttered her room.

"I don't have a good feeling about Luna," Miss Elva announced, coming in from the kitchen, carrying a few pouches that she shoved into her cross-body leather satchel. Today she wore a long caftan in muted purple, looking positively demure by her standards.

"Where's Rafe?" I asked.

"I sent him out to do some searching for me. He can get into places unseen that I can't," Miss Elva explained, smoothing back her hair, which today was unleashed in a riot of ringlets and held back with a jeweled headband.

"Smart," I said, then stopped at the front door.

"Cash is in the car. My…boyfriend," I said, pausing to think about what I wanted to say.

"And you don't want me say anything too crazy to scare him off," Miss Elva said, waving her hand in the air. "Child, I know."

"Please don't be offended, it's not like that. You know I love you," I protested, immediately feeling guilty. "I just want to kind of ease him into all this magickal stuff. He's not used to this world."

Miss Elva shot me a glance, her hands on her hips.

"And you're gonna hide yourself from him? I don't know if I hold with that, now." She was right, but I didn't want to get into it at the moment.

"No, I'm not hiding. We just haven't been together long enough for him to learn it all at once. This is still pretty new to him," I said.

"Well, he'll learn soon enough. We'll just have to see

how he weathers the storm," Miss Elva said, breezing past me and onto the porch.

I wasn't sure if I liked what that meant, but I was unwilling to leave Miss Elva alone with Cash for long, so I dashed after her and opened the front door of Cash's Jeep for her.

"Cash, this is the esteemed Miss Elva, the best voodoo priestess in Florida," I said, meeting her eyes to let her know I wasn't trying to hide what she was from Cash.

Miss Elva harrumphed and then slid into the front seat, reaching out a hand to Cash.

"That's in *all* the States, honey, and don't let Miss Marie in N'awlins tell you any different," she said, settling in comfortably.

I saw Cash's lips quirk and I blew out a breath.

"I'm sure you're the best at what you do," Cash said magnanimously, and pulled away from the curb.

"Where are we going first?" I asked.

"I've got to get Dylan. He's been kicking his heels at the coffee shop waiting on me," Cash said, and I immediately felt bad.

"I'm sorry, I didn't even think about that," I said, immediately chagrined and a little embarrassed. Now Dylan was going to get caught up in our little drama and I could only imagine what Cash's mama was going to hear about me.

One thing at a time, I reminded myself. We needed to figure out where Luna was.

"When's the last time you heard from Luna?" Miss Elva asked, turning to look at me.

"She texted to check on me earlier today, but since

then it's been silence. And her phone's going to voicemail, which never happens because of Granny Lavelle up at Seashores."

Miss Elva nodded, not saying anything.

The houses of Tequila Key flashed by my window, all cluttered together, clambering for space on this scrap of land in the Keys. I prayed that Luna wasn't going to be the third dead body to end up at that beach.

Something niggled in the back of my mind, but just as I was grasping at it, we pulled onto the main drag and I saw Dylan leaning against the front wall of Beau's new restaurant, talking animatedly to Beau.

"Looks like Dylan has already met Beau," I said, smiling as I saw them both laugh at the same time. They'd make a handsome couple, all bronzed and well-dressed.

"Damn it. I wanted to be the one to introduce them. Leave it to Dylan to steal my thunder," Cash griped, swinging the car into a spot right in front of the restaurant. The men looked over and smiled at us as we got out of the Jeep.

"Hi, Beau," I said, smiling when he came over to pull me into a hug.

"Can you believe how freakin' hot Dylan is?" Beau hissed into my ear, and my smile grew even wider as I looked up at Beau.

"Trust me, I get it," I replied, and Beau shook his head in disbelief before turning to hug Miss Elva.

"Child, I've been meaning to come look at the renovations," Miss Elva said after being introduced to Dylan, who looked at her curiously but refrained from commenting.

"Yes, please, come in. Sorry it's such a mess in here, but it's still a construction zone," Beau explained, ushering us in and locking the door behind us. "Sorry to lock the door, but you know how the looky-loo's are in this town. I swear Prudie hovers outside the front door, just waiting for a glimpse inside." Beau gestured to where he had tacked up brown butcher paper over all the windows and the glass doors to prevent prying eyes from seeing inside.

"That woman is on my list," I declared.

"Your hit list or your shit list?" Beau joked, then stiffened when I glared at him. The last thing I needed was for Dylan to think I actually went around trying to kill people.

"My shit list. She's a mean old gossip," I said, then turned to look at the space. "Holy crap, you've done a ton of work since I was last in here."

The restaurant that had originally been Luca's Deli had transformed from a small deli with a long counter and glass food case on one wall to a sleek, elegant, and slightly edgy restaurant. Beau had removed the counters, knocked out the back wall and added a second-floor kitchen. What had once been the back stockroom was now a wall of windows, opening the entire room to a view of cerulean blue waves crashing against a rocky beach.

"Beau, this is fantastic," I breathed, walking around to look at the newly added second floor. "The second floor doesn't even cut into the space at all."

"Right? I really wanted to add that view. Plus, with moving the kitchen upstairs, I was able to get the view and add a small eating area outside as well," Beau said.

"So will the waiters have to run up and downstairs with

trays of food?" I asked, knowing that if I was tasked with that job, I'd be dropping trays left and right.

I may be a wee bit klutzy.

"Nope, get this," Beau said, leading me back to where a wall, about a foot taller than my head, separated an area of the room. Behind it, I found a serving station for drinks and a huge dumbwaiter tucked into the wall.

"A dumbwaiter! Makes total sense," I said, approving it.

"I can't wait to get into the design palette, but first the construction needed to be finished. I meant to ask you… could I commission you for the art? I want only your underwater photographs on the wall. But like huge…going all the way up the wall."

I brought my hand to my mouth, surprised and flattered that he would want my photographs in his elegant restaurant.

"Really? You want my pictures in here? I don't know if they're good enough," I began and Beau hushed me with a finger on my lips.

"They're stunning. I just am going to have to decide if I want to do all black and white or if I want to do color," Beau mused as we walked around the wall and back towards where the rest of the group was standing.

"Color what?" Cash asked.

"I want Althea's underwater photography on the walls. Huge," Beau said, gesturing at the walls.

"That's a great idea, she has a fantastic eye," Cash agreed and I turned to him, surprised.

"Really?"

"Really. I was going to commission a few of your

pieces for a club in Miami too, but haven't had a chance to bring it up. We've been a little distracted today," Cash reminded me.

Oh crap. Luna.

"Yeah, so, uh, what was that all about this morning, if you don't mind me asking?" There was a slightly aggressive edge to Dylan's tone, and Beau immediately planted his hand on his hips.

"What are you talking about?"

"Chief Thomas pulled me in for questioning on those murders," I quickly explained to Beau before he got snarky with Dylan. I didn't want him to ruin a potential love match because of me.

"Why did he pull you in?" Beau asked, swinging back to me.

"Because Luna and I had been at the beach the night before they found the dead body," I admitted and I saw Dylan shake his head.

"Well, that doesn't mean squat," Beau said, always on my side.

"I know. Which is why I'm here and not under arrest. At least this sheriff is better than our last one," I pointed out. Beau rolled his eyes and nodded in agreement.

"We've got a major problem though," I began, shooting a glance at Dylan before turning back to Beau.

"What's wrong?" Beau asked, immediately running his hands up and down my arms to soothe me.

"They found another body over in the same area this morning, and Luna's missing now too." The words rushed out and Beau stiffened.

"How do you know she's missing?"

"Her phone's turned off."

"That never happens," Beau said immediately and I nodded.

"Who's Luna?" Dylan asked, looking between us.

"Our best friend," Beau and I answered simultaneously.

My phone beeped from my purse, and I raced across the room to where I had dropped it on a small table.

"This is probably her now, and we'll have been worried over nothing," I called over my shoulder.

Pulling my phone from my bag, I swiped to read the text.

Chills raced through me and I almost dropped the phone. Horrified, I looked up helplessly at Cash.

"Luna's been taken."

Chapter Thirty-One

THE ROOM EXPLODED with questions from everyone and I held up my hand to stop them.

"Listen, it says – I have Luna. Meet us at North Beach at sundown. Bring the voodoo priestess. Come alone or I'll snap Luna's neck." I shivered at the words and looked helplessly at Beau.

"What number did it come from?" Miss Elva asked, shaking her head.

"Luna's," I said.

"Can we trace it? If it's on?" Miss Elva asked.

Cash thought about it and then instructed me to call Luna. It went straight to voicemail and I just shook my head helplessly.

"You are not going to that beach," Cash ordered, testosterone oozing off of him as he looked at me, hands clenched.

"Oh, I most certainly am going," I seethed, squaring off with him.

"You are not. If you think I'm going to let you go alone

to a beach to face some psychopath, you're insane," Cash argued.

"If you think I'll just sit around and let my best friend be held captive by said psychopath, then you're the crazy one," I argued right back.

"You're not going, and that's final," Cash ordered.

My phone rang and I turned my attention back to it, shooting a death glare at Cash.

"Hello?"

"Thea, it's Trace. What's going on?" His worried voice sounded through the phone and I realized I'd forgotten to call him like I'd promised.

"It's Trace," I said to the group, then turned away, not caring if I was annoying Cash.

"They found another dead body. And now Luna's been kidnapped." I explained things as briefly as possible, as recounting the story made my stomach turn.

"What do you need me to do?" Trace asked immediately.

"They asked that Miss Elva and I come to the beach alone tonight. Cash says he won't let me," I raised my voice and saw Cash shoot me a glare.

"That guy," Trace complained.

"I can't leave Luna," I explained.

I heard Trace sigh on the other end of the line. There was a moment of silence, then he asked me something that made my mouth drop open. Holding the phone away from me, I turned to Cash.

"He wants to speak with you," I said, handing the phone out and moving to stand by Beau.

"Well, well, well. This gets more and more interesting," Beau whispered in my ear and I elbowed him in the gut, trying to listen to what Cash was saying into the phone.

"Sounds like a plan. See you at sunset. I'll call Chief Thomas," Cash said and then hung up the phone, handing it back to me wordlessly.

"Well?" I demanded, refusing to be cut out of the situation.

Cash sighed and ran his hand through his hair, looking sexy and frustrated, momentarily distracting me as I watched the muscles in his arm ripple.

"Stay on point, girl," Beau whispered to me.

Right, focus.

I shook my head and waited for Cash to speak.

"You and Miss Elva will drive to the beach. Trace, Chief Thomas, and I will take Trace's boat with no running lights and approach the beach from the water using the electric motor."

"I'm coming too," Beau said at the same time as Dylan. The two men looked at each other appreciatively for a moment.

"Stay on point, girl," I whispered to Beau, and he smacked my arm.

"Fine, whatever, I don't care. You go by land, we'll go by water, and that's it," Cash declared.

"Okay." Miss Elva finally spoke and then turned to meet my eyes. "Althea, you're coming home with me. We've got some planning to do."

"Four hours until sunset," Cash said, looking at the time on his phone.

"Go team?" I said weakly, and Beau just shook his head at me as Cash's brow furrowed even more deeply.

Well, Sunday evening was sure looking up. So much for those cuddles on the couch with Cash I had been looking forward to.

Chapter Thirty-Two

CASH DROPPED US off at my house, pulling me in for a fierce kiss before letting me go.

"Don't do anything stupid tonight," Cash ordered, pressing his forehead against mine as he looked in my eyes.

"I would never do anything stupid," I insisted, and Miss Elva snorted behind me.

"Yeah, that's what I thought," Cash grumbled.

"Hey, it'll be okay. We can handle this," I said softly pulling away from Cash and running my hand down his cheek. "Just, well, take whatever happens tonight with a grain of salt."

"What's that supposed to mean?" Cash asked, clearly annoyed with me.

I pointed between Miss Elva and myself, raising an eyebrow at Cash.

"You may see something unusual. We don't really accomplish things in a normal way, get what I'm saying?"

Cash's eyes flitted over to where Miss Elva stood watching us and back to my face.

"I see."

Cash was going to have to get used to the weird things that happened when I was around. Plain and simple.

I think he realized that as he nodded and dropped another kiss on my lips.

"Just add a layer of magick or whatever to make bullets bounce off of you, okay? I'd like for us to get back to my original evening plans," Cash said.

"Me too," I breathed, feeling my heart pick up its pace as I lost myself for a second in his eyes.

"Althea. Focus," Miss Elva ordered and I shook my head.

"Sorry, sorry. Go, you need to leave," I all but shoved Cash into the car, my cheeks flushed with embarrassment and lust.

"Stay in contact," Cash ordered.

"Aye, aye, Captain," I said, saluting smartly before rolling my eyes at myself and turning back to Miss Elva.

She just shook her head at me, her curls bouncing around her shoulders.

"Child, you gonna have to learn how to keep it cool around that man of yours."

"It's hard. Have you seen him?"

"I have two eyes in my head now, don't I?"

I stopped on my porch and thought about what we needed to do for the rest of the day, anxiety already creeping up my spine as I thought about Luna being held by a lunatic.

"Do you want to stay here or go to your house?" I asked Miss Elva.

"My house. I have more tools there," Miss Elva said.

"Let me let Hank out and then we'll go."

Hank had already seen us; his ears were bouncing up and down below the front windowsill. I knew I'd break his heart if I just left again without coming in to see him.

We stepped inside and Hank danced around my feet before catching wind of Miss Elva. He immediately stopped his bouncing and sniffed at the hem of her caftan before rolling over on his back, his paws in the air.

"Whoa, what did you do to him?" I asked, amazed at the complacency that Hank was displaying.

Miss Elva just smiled and bent over to scratch Hank's tummy, and if that dog could have died of bliss right there, he would have. I actually felt a little jealous, but wasn't going to admit it.

"Nothing, child. Animals love me."

"Is that so? Are you like a dog whisperer?" I asked, moving across the room to slide the back door open.

"Something like that. Child, I'd change into something darker than what you're wearing now," Miss Elva said and I glanced down at my white dress.

"You're absolutely right. I don't even know what I was thinking buying a white dress to begin with," I grumbled, taking the stairs two at a time to my bedroom.

"It looks nice against your skin tone, though," Miss Elva called up the steps.

It wouldn't look that nice with blood on it, I thought, worried about what would happen that evening. I pulled the dress off over my head and threw it on my bed, and tugged a serviceable black maxi dress from my closet and tugged it on over my head.

I like maxi dresses, okay?

Taking my earrings out as well, I tossed them on top of the dress on the bed and pulled my curls into a loose bun on the top of my head.

It was time to kick a little ass.

Sliding my feet back in my Toms, I all but ran downstairs, knowing that time was at a premium if Miss Elva was to get one of her potions or powders ready. I stopped by my dive bag and dug out the pouch that Miss Elva had given me earlier, tucking it in my bra for safekeeping. I'd already learned how quickly you could be divested of your purse or other belongings, so bra it was for safekeeping.

"Is this okay?" I asked Miss Elva, who sat on the back porch throwing a ball for Hank. "Black dress, no jewelry, and shoes I can run in?"

"I don't know who you think is going to be doing any running, child, but it sho ain't gonna be me," Miss Elva said, heaving herself off the couch and whistling once to Hank, who immediately dropped his ball and ran to her side.

"Who is this dog of mine? Usually I have to battle with him to get him to drop that damn ball," I asked, side-eying Hank as we went inside. That little traitor'd known how to drop all along.

"You just gotta talk to him in a language he knows," Miss Elva said, bending to pat Hank once on the head while he sat, his boxy head tilted, his tongue lolling out as he looked at Miss Elva with adoration.

"It's like he doesn't even know me," I grumbled,

pulling a toy out and tossing it across the room. Hank didn't even move, just continued to sit and stare up at Miss Elva. "This is ridiculous. Let's go."

I was more than a little miffed that my dog had chosen Miss Elva over me and I stayed silent as I left the house, carefully locking the door and controlling my urge to stomp to the car.

"Child, no need to get jealous. All dogs are like that with me. Not just Hank. They just know I love them."

"Hank knows I love him," I pointed out as we pulled onto the street.

"Of course he does. It's just the newness of me. You have to understand that I'm old magick. I'm more than Voodoo. I'm all connected, child. I'm in tune with this earth and all its animals. Hank can't help but love me," Miss Elva said.

Huh. Well, that was certainly some food for thought.

"I'm sorry. I think I just have a lot of anxiety right now. I'm worried about Luna. I'm worried about rescuing her tonight. I'm not the best at covert operations, if you didn't know," I pointed out as I pulled my car to a stop in front of Miss Elva's house.

The late afternoon sun warmed the street, casting its glow against the brightly colored houses, while puffy clouds wafted through a blue sky. It was another perfect day in paradise and I was about to go track a killer.

How could things get any worse?

Chapter Thirty-Three

"I'VE ALWAYS WANTED to spend some time in your house," I admitted as Miss Elva ushered me through her main living room and back to her gleamingly clean kitchen, where a butcher block island sat in the middle.

"Sit," Miss Elva ordered, immediately moving to where an apron hung on a hook and pulling it over her head.

Miss Elva didn't talk to me – instead she opened a door and stepped into a pantry while I looked around her kitchen. It was fairly small as kitchens go, but unless you're a millionaire you aren't getting a huge kitchen in houses in the Florida Keys. It's just the way it works down here. You pay a high price for square footage, but nobody complains because you spend most of your time outside anyway.

Miss Elva's kitchen was done up in a soothing buttercup yellow and cream motif, with pots and pans hanging from hooks overhead and a Haitian-style art piece in dramatic colors on the wall. Overall, by the kitchen you'd never know that a Voodoo priestess lived here, as opposed to the craziness that existed in her front room. I wondered at the dichotomy of it.

"Miss Elva, why does your kitchen not look like your living room?" I asked, and Miss Elva poked her head out of the pantry.

"The kitchen is where I work. You don't see a surgeon going into a messy operating room, do you?"

Hard to argue with that logic.

Miss Elva came out of the pantry carrying a brown wicker basket with jars piled high and several small burlap bags.

"What are you going to make?"

"I'm not quite sure what I'm going to use yet, so we're going in fully stocked," Miss Elva said.

She opened another cabinet and pulled out a mortar and pestle, sliding it across the butcher-block island at me. She rooted around in her basket for a while before pulling out a jar of red flakes.

"Grind this. Counter-clockwise. Breathe through your mouth," Miss Elva ordered.

"All of it?" I asked, holding the jar up to the light and shaking it gently.

"All of it; now hush, child, I need to focus," Miss Elva said, hefting her weight onto a stool as she began to pull items from the basket and lay them in front of her. I noticed pieces of straw, small Popsicle sticks, twine, scraps of fabric, and a variety of jars full of roots and leaves.

"What are you making?" I asked and Miss Elva sighed dramatically.

"Did I stutter? Is there something making you unable

to understand the words 'hush, child'? Do I need to repeat myself?"

"No, ma'am," I said, turning back to my task. Now I was even more curious but, knowing she'd kick me off my stool if I said another word, I opened my jar and poured the contents gently into the small stone bowl, being careful to breathe through my mouth as Miss Elva had instructed. Picking up the pestle, I began to grind the red flakes counter-clockwise, losing myself in the hypnotic rhythm of the grinding motion and trying not to let my worries for Luna consume me.

"That's good," Miss Elva's voice interrupted my thoughts and I realized that I'd ground the little red flakes into a fine dust. "Pour it in this pouch."

I did as I was told and handed Miss Elva the pouch, wondering what would happen next. I was surprised to see that she had constructed a little man of sorts in front of her; the wrists and ankles were tied together, the mouth gagged and eyes blindfolded. She was slowly stuffing herbs into the body of the doll.

"You're making a voodoo doll? What are you stuffing inside it?"

"Confusion herbs. Valerian. Wormwood and the like," Miss Elva said, concentrating on the task at hand. I didn't want to interrupt her process, so for once in my life I remained quiet, while she finished stitching the little doll closed. When she was done, she looked at it for a moment, nodding to herself before turning to me.

"Go ahead, ask your questions," Miss Elva said, getting up to pour herself a glass of water.

"I just...I thought voodoo dolls only worked if you had

a piece of hair or a cigarette butt or something from the person you're trying to control," I said, resting my elbows on the counter as I studied the doll.

"You're absolutely right. That's usually what's needed," Miss Elva said, finishing her water with a sigh.

"But you don't need that?"

"Child, I told you I was old magick. Sure, some of the newer priestesses starting out will need those physical bits to tie the magick to the doll, but I'm stronger than that. All I need is my intent." Miss Elva smiled at me.

"So why use the doll at all? Couldn't you just cast a spell without it?"

"I might do that too. I don't know what we're walking into. I prefer to have all my tools with me. You don't go to a gun fight carrying a spatula now, do you?"

I refrained from pointing out that we were going to a potential gunfight and all she was bringing was a doll.

See? I do have a sense of self-preservation sometimes.

"You go on out on the porch now. I have to run some charms on these pouches and I don't want your thoughts interfering," Miss Elva said.

"Fine by me, I could use some fresh air anyway," I said. I walked through Miss Elva's living room, restraining myself from stopping to peer at all the curiosities on her shelves, and made my way to the uncomfortable visitor's chair on Miss Elva's front porch. Even though she wasn't sitting on the porch with me, I still knew better than to sit in Miss Elva's rocking chair.

"Althea," a voice said at my shoulder, and I swear I almost jumped three feet out of that chair.

"Damn it, Rafe! I told you not to do that," I hissed,

throwing my hand over my heart as I gave the pirate an evil look.

"Sorry, I forget you can't sense me," Rafe admitted, coming to float in front of me.

"Did you find anything out? Did you see Luna?"

"Luna? Why would I be looking for the witch? I thought I was supposed to go look for that crazy horn-wearing Pagan guy?"

That's right. Rafe hadn't been with us when we'd discovered Luna had been taken.

"Luna was kidnapped. Presumably by the killer. We have to go to the beach tonight and rescue her," I explained.

Rafe stood tall and saluted me.

"I will protect my queen at all costs," Rafe intoned.

"Well, yes, and maybe me too?" I offered, annoyed that he seemed to have forgotten all about me.

"You too – you're not so bad," Rafe said.

"Gee, thanks Rafe. Tell me what happened out at the festival?"

"Nothing, actually. I searched for a really long time. It's like there was never a festival there at all." Rafe shrugged.

"Really? No fire pit? No battened down grass? No litter? No tents?" I fired off questions at Rafe and he just continued to shake his head no.

"Honestly, nothing. I backtracked and then made sure that I had gone to the right spot, because it looked as though nothing had been there. But I finally found some confirmation of the festival."

"What was that?"

"There's sort of an energy portal that has been opened up. It must have been where the crazy dude called on the powers."

This was not good.

"An energy portal? Like a passageway to hell?"

Rafe shrugged.

"Maybe, maybe not? It's not huge. Just a bit of pulsing energy there. Something to keep an eye on, for sure. Especially with All Hallows' Eve next month."

Fantastic. An energy portal opened up to the underworld right before Halloween. I'm sure nothing bad will happen with that. At all.

Rubbing my hands over my face, I breathed deeply for a moment.

"One thing at a time here, Rafe. We have to get Luna. Then we'll deal with the energy portal."

Rafe shrugged his shoulders. He had all the time in the world.

I jumped as a ripple of energy ran through the house, powerful magick pressing against the back of me and causing the hairs on the back of my neck to stand up.

"I love when she uses magick, it's so sexy," Rafe breathed, his eyes wide as he peered into the house.

"Yes, super sexy," I said as the front door cracked open and Miss Elva poked her head out.

"What are we doing about dinner?" she demanded.

"Dinner? I don't know if I can eat," I admitted.

"I passed a food truck on the way over here," Rafe said helpfully. Miss Elva met my eyes.

"Go get us food. Rafe, you go with her," she instructed as the door slammed behind her.

"Isn't she great?" Rafe enthused by my side as I walked down the block and turned onto the next street.

"Yes, a real dreamboat," I said, keeping my wits about me as I scanned the pedestrians cycling and walking by, looking for anything out of order. The food truck was parked on a corner and advertised take-away Mexican food; the spicy scents wafting from it made my mouth water. Food trucks had become all the rage in the Keys about five or ten years ago, and it seemed like we had a new one come through every week.

After ordering two platters of steak and chicken fajitas, I made my way back to Miss Elva's to find her on the front porch, a satchel by her side.

"Sun's close to setting. Let's eat and get going. Rafe, did you find anything out today?"

Rafe hung his head in apology.

"I did not. Only that an energy portal seems to have been opened."

Miss Elva whipped her head up at that news, then speared a piece of steak with her fork.

"Why is it that I have to take care of everything that goes wrong in this town?" she muttered to herself.

"Because you're the boss queen of the world?" I asked, being more than slightly sarcastic.

Miss Elva pointed her fork at me.

"And don't you forget it."

Chapter Thirty-Four

"I LITERALLY HATE THIS," I complained as I crept the car along the gravel path towards the beach. The sun had just set, leaving us in the shadow of twilight as we bumped down the gravel road towards the beach. I'd kept my lights on, because, well, why try to hide? We'd been invited – that is, ordered – to come to the beach.

My anxiety was running at about a ten, so I took a few deep breaths to calm myself.

"Don't you worry, child, that Horace has nothing on us," Miss Elva said soothingly.

"Except for the fact that he's opened a portal to hell and has, like, demonic power now. You know, no big deal," I muttered, and Miss Elva chuckled next to me.

"You think this is the first demon Miss Elva's had to show what's what? Child, please," Miss Elva clucked her tongue at me and I had to smile.

I mean, if I had to battle a demon, I'd pick Miss Elva at my side any day.

We drove as far along the lane as we could, almost

reaching the beach. Remembering how Luna had faced the car out the other night, I did a quick three point turn in the small lane and pointed the car back towards the road. Miss Elva nodded her approval and then we got out of the car, Rafe bringing up the rear.

The ocean was quiet tonight, the tide having just finished coming in. A light breeze brushed against me, bringing that salty swampy smell of saltwater with it, and I reached out to grab Miss Elva's hand as we stepped onto the empty beach.

I couldn't believe I was doing this. Just putting myself out there to get shot in the chest. As soon as the thought came to me, I invoked my white bubble of protection and slammed it down over Miss Elva and myself, just in case.

A pinging sound brought my head up and I jumped as something seemed to ripple in the air and then breeze past me.

"What was that?" I gasped.

"Someone just shot at us. Your little protective bubble is holding up nicely. I'm impressed," Miss Elva nodded easily and I wanted to scream at her.

Someone had just shot at us and Miss Elva was complimenting my magick?

Miss Elva turned to the empty beach, facing the direction the bullets had come from.

"I know you didn't just try and shoot at us. You'll have to do better than that. Why don't you show yourself, you coward? You asked us to come here; well, we're here."

"Oh, that's good. I'm sure calling a killer a coward is going to make him more amenable to handing Luna off," I swore, keeping a hold on that protective bubble as we stepped forward.

Another ping and I jumped again as my protective bubble rippled. I noticed this was all happening on my side of the bubble – now I was mad.

"Oh, so it's just me you want to kill? Right, that's great – right sporting of you," I yelled at the bushes. "Can't you do something here, Miss Elva? I'm kind of busy stopping bullets in mid-air," I griped. Jeez, bring a voodoo priestess to a fight and she just antagonizes the killer.

Miss Elva cast me a look and then dug in her satchel, pulling out a small bag. She dumped powder onto her hand and then, closing her eyes, blew it gently from her palm.

"Illuminate," she whispered.

The powder seemed to sparkle of its own accord, wafting on the breeze across the beach, and settling onto the sand and the bushes. I gasped; in moments, the entire beach was lit up brighter than a football field. I turned to Miss Elva in admiration.

"Good one," I said, nodding at her.

"I try," Miss Elva said, smirking as we drew closer to where we could now see a man standing next to a body on the sand. My heart jumped in my throat to see a swath of Luna's bright blonde hair in the sand, but then I saw her leg move and realized that she was still alive. Thank the Goddess.

My eyes landed on the killer and I gasped. I had been expecting it to be Horace, had even prepared for it to be Horace, but it was truly the last person that I had expected.

Confusion filled me as I met his eyes.

Chapter Thirty-Five

"I DON'T UNDERSTAND," I said.

"Nobody listens. Nobody ever listens. It doesn't matter if I file with the Conservation Office. It doesn't matter if I file with the Fish and Wildlife Office. Nobody cares. Well, now they're going to care," the man seethed, a gun in each hand as he paced.

It was the dreadlocked environmentalist that I had seen that night outside Lucky's, handing off fliers about saving the turtles to patrons as they waited in line. I'd thought he was a little overzealous at the time, but I'd missed the fact that he was a complete lunatic.

Maybe it was time for me to start paying a little more attention to others.

"What are you going on about?" Miss Elva demanded, surprising the man into stopping his rant as he sized her up.

"The turtles," he said slowly, keeping his eyes trained on her.

"And what do the turtles have to do with killing honest people and shooting at us?" Miss Elva demanded.

"The turtles lay their eggs on this beach. If the condo development gets built here, there will be no place for them to go," the man said.

"Who are you?" I cut in.

"Darius Masterson. I'm a biologist," Darius explained, the guns still trained on us.

"Darius, don't you think there might be a better way to accomplish all this?" I asked gently.

"I tried. I really tried. For a year now. Nobody cares. They take my fliers and throw them away. Nobody listens," Darius said, his dreadlocks sticking out like crazy and bouncing around his head while he shouted.

"Why did you want us to come here tonight?"

"I only wanted the voodoo priestess. Not the psychic. She can't do anything," Darius scoffed. I felt offended.

"Excuse me? I can do plenty of things," I said, hand on hip. Miss Elva cast me a look and I shut up. I wondered if Cash was on the boat watching all this, and if they were planning to take a shot at Darius. Considering the possibility, I slowly began to move closer to Miss Elva, positioning ourselves so that we weren't blocking the sightline from the water.

"I want you to put a curse on this beach," Darius demanded of Miss Elva, and she nodded slowly, listening to him.

"What did you do to Luna?" I asked, my eyes on my best friend on the ground. She was laid out with her back to us, but I could see her arm move a little, so I knew she was still breathing.

"I just knocked her out, she's fine," Darius said, dismissing her.

"How come you took Luna?" Miss Elva demanded.

"I heard she was a witch. But she told me she doesn't do curses and that I had to get Miss Elva."

Luna was smart, that's for sure.

"What was with the whole drilling the saplings in that guy's head, then?" I said, keeping him talking and trying desperately not to glance towards the water to see if the boat was near. At least they would be able to see clearly, thanks to Miss Elva's charm.

"Wasn't that great? I knew the Pagan festival was in town; then when I saw you guys doing your ritual on the beach, I figured it would be a perfect spot to lay the body out. It looked really cool, if I do say so myself," Darius puffed out his chest a bit, seeming very proud of himself.

"Yeah, super cool. So you watched our whole ritual?" I wondered if he knew about Rafe, who was currently flitting around Miss Elva's head. I tried not to get grossed out thinking about Darius creeping around in the bushes while we were skyclad on the beach.

"Nah, I just caught the end. It was pretty cool. That's why I wanted to take Luna. She clearly knew what she was doing. You on the other hand...well, you need some work."

Don't get offended, don't get offended. I was tempted to toss some power at this dude to see what he would do, but with one gun trained on Luna's inert body and the other on us, I felt like my hands were tied.

"Sure, I'll put a curse on the beach for you. I just need

to get my stuff out of my bag," Miss Elva said, holding her hands up and explaining what she was going to do.

"Any weird moves and I'll shoot this one," Darius said, gesturing with a gun at Luna. I shivered.

"This is the police! Put your hands in the air!"

I was so shocked by the voice that thundered over the megaphone that I dropped my mental shield.

Which proved to be a critical mistake when Darius grabbed me and dragged me in front of his body, pulling me further out onto the beach so I blocked him entirely from the boat that rocked gently in the water in front of us. Darius hadn't seen them yet.

I closed my eyes as cool steel brushed my forehead.

This wasn't exactly how I had planned for things to go tonight. In fact, I was supposed to be curled up on my couch with Cash and Hank right at this very moment. I gulped as I felt tears slip into my eyes.

The cold steel of the gun slipped past my face and fell to the ground. It was all I could do not to jerk forward and try to pick it up.

"What's happening?" Darius screeched into my ear, and I winced at the sound. He began to keen and wail into my ear, rendering me all but deaf. I gasped as his arm tightened for a moment around my throat, cutting off my supply of air. The wails increased in fervency, until his arms loosened around me and I gasped as, suddenly, I was free. Without thinking, I ran to where Luna lay huddled on the ground, praying I wasn't about to take a bullet in the back.

Risking a glance, I looked back.

Darius danced around the beach, still holding one gun in a hand, both hands to his head while he screamed. I cast a glance at Miss Elva to see her holding the doll in one hand.

Having learned from my previous mistakes, I kept my mouth shut, huddling over Luna as I ripped through the duct tape that was wrapped around her arms and legs.

Miss Elva twisted the doll's neck and Darius doubled over, coughing and choking, scrambling at his throat with his hands, his nails leaving red marks as he tore at his skin. Out of the corner of my eye, I saw Chief Thomas hop from the boat and race across the beach, tackling Darius easily and pressing his face into the sand.

In moments, Darius was cuffed and I stared in awe as Miss Elva slipped the little doll back into her satchel.

"Miss Elva, that was something…" I trailed off. I didn't really even have the words for witnessing something like that. I get a little speechless when I'm in the presence of major power.

Luna moaned softly and I turned back to her as people jumped from the boat and flooded the beach.

"Luna," I gasped, wincing at the duct tape that covered her mouth, knowing I would hurt her if I ripped it from her delicate skin. Her eyelashes fluttered against her smooth skin, before opening to look at me. Confusion crossed her features for a moment before she focused on my face and understood I was here to help her.

"Luna, I have to pull this duct tape off. It's going to hurt like a bitch. I'm so sorry," I said, reaching out to touch the corner of the tape on her face. Luna nodded, understanding what needed to be done.

"Here, child, let me handle this," Miss Elva said, maneuvering me aside and dipping into what I was now forever going to refer to as her magickal satchel. She pulled out a tube of some kind of ointment and ran it across the edges of the tape, taking care not to get any in Luna's nostrils. Once she was done, she capped the bottle, laid her hand over the duct tape, and pulled gently.

The tape came off easily in one piece. There wasn't even a mark on Luna's face.

"Damn, yo. You should sell that," I said to Miss Elva before leaning over to hug Luna.

"I was so scared," I whispered into her hair, holding her tightly. Luna was more than just a best friend, she was like a sister to me. Imagining my life without her –well, I just couldn't go there right now. Luna's body began to shake in the aftermath and I ran my hands down her arms, sending a little soothing energy into her. She smiled her thanks at me.

"I was scared too. I honestly never would have thought the killer was the hippie environmentalist dude," Luna said, casting a look over at the beach.

"You're telling me."

We all watched as Chief Thomas read Darius his rights. Beau and Cash turned away once they saw that everything was kosher with Chief Thomas, and raced across the sand to us.

"Luna!" Beau said, dropping to his knees in the sand and hugging her.

"Sure, don't mind me, I'm fine too," I grumbled at Beau, then gasped as I was scooped off the ground and pressed to Cash's muscular chest.

Can we pause to appreciate the strength of a man who can lift a grown woman from the ground?

His lips found mine, and everything just fell away for a while. I sighed into his mouth, snuggling into his warmth and solidness, wanting to stay there just a moment longer.

A throat cleared behind us and Cash broke his kiss, though he didn't turn.

"Please don't do that to me again. I don't know if my heart can take it," Cash said seriously, his grey eyes clouded with concern.

"Yes, I'd ideally not want to go through something like that again," I agreed, before Cash let my feet down and I slid down his body.

His muscular hard body.

Shaking my head to focus, I peeked around Cash's arm to see Dylan standing there.

"Sorry, Dylan. I know this wasn't what you were expecting to do today," I said.

"No problem, just glad to see everyone is okay," Dylan said, coming to stand by Beau and lending a hand to pull Luna to a standing position.

"We've got to go back on the boat to get to our car. Are you guys okay to leave from here?" Cash asked. I turned to look out at where Trace idled the boat in front of the beach. I could just barely make him out in the glow from Miss Elva's charm, and I waved to him, wanting to thank him for his help. When I saw his hand shoot up in response, I breathed a sigh of relief.

"I just don't understand," I heard Dylan saying as he walked around, trying to figure out the source of the light. Beau clapped him on the shoulder and shook his head.

"Best not to ask too many questions. You'll learn that pretty quickly if you come down here more often."

And wasn't that just the truth of it?

Chapter Thirty-Six

"I CAN'T BELIEVE the environmentalist was the killer," Luna said. All of us girls were in the car, heading back towards downtown Tequila. I'd agreed to drop Miss Elva and Luna off at Lucky's, while I was going to stop at home and meet up with Cash for our promised date.

"I could have told you that," Rafe's voice was filled with scorn, and we all whipped our heads around to look at where he sat in the back seat.

"What do you mean, you could have told us that?" I asked, annoyance lacing my tone.

"I knew he was the killer," Rafe said slowly, like it was no big deal.

"Well, why didn't you say something then?" Luna protested.

Rafe shrugged.

"Nobody asked me."

And there you have it, folks. Apparently ghosts take everything literally and you have to be very specific with them.

"You've got to be kidding me, Rafe. What did you think we were doing all this time?" I asked.

"I don't know. I wasn't around half the time you were hunting for the killer. I thought you wanted me to find Horace, anyway."

"That's all right, sweetie. We'll just know to clarify things with you in the future," Miss Elva soothed and Rafe looked at her, his expression dripping in adoration and love.

"Gag me," I muttered.

"Now, no need to be angry, child. All's well that ends well. We're all safe. You've got your man, life is good," Miss Elva scolded me as I pulled to a stop by Lucky's.

"Yeah, well, I don't really know if I've got my man. He seemed pretty shaken up by all this magick stuff. And his brother is certainly going to have a story to tell his whole family too," I said wearily.

Luna squeezed my shoulder sympathetically as she got out of the car.

"Cash is a good guy. Just talk to him about this stuff. Don't keep him in the dark. I'm sure he'll be fine with all of it."

"Thanks, friend. I'm just happy nothing worse happened to you."

"I'm good. It was scary when he kidnapped me, but I'm okay now. Just a bump on the head. Now, I just really want some food," Luna said.

Miss Elva looked at me for a moment from the front seat.

"Don't you hide yourself from that man. If he doesn't know what he's got, that's his own damn fault," she said before heaving herself out of the front seat and onto the side of the road.

Tough to argue with that. I suppose a lot of things in life and love come down to showing people your true colors. And learning to understand that you can't control how they will respond to you. That's what makes love such a tricky thing. You both rip open those doors to your insides and show each other your goods, like you're peddling your wares. Sure you shine it up real nice, but we all know that a frying pan is a frying pan. We just need to find the person who is looking for a new frying pan, is all.

I shook my head as I parked the car, surprised to feel a wave of melancholy wash over me as I trudged up the steps. Perhaps being deeply introspective about life wasn't the best thing for me to do at the moment. Didn't we all just want to be loved and accepted?

My thoughts distracted me from the fact that Hank's ears weren't poking over the edge of the windowsill.

I opened the door and immediately crouched down to pet Hank.

Except there was no Hank to be seen.

What the heck?

"Hank?"

Worry ratcheted through me as my eyes darted around the room, looking for Hank.

Finally I saw him. His body was stretched out flat and his nose was pressed to the window, his hackles raised. A low growl emitted from his throat and he didn't even look away to glance back at me.

So, you know, not a typical welcome home.

My backyard was dark and the switch for the light was

right next to the back door. If I crossed the room and turned it on, I would reveal myself to whatever Hank was growling at.

See, here's the part about me not being so great in emergencies. What I probably should have done was gone back outside and called Cash. Instead, I strode right across the living room and flashed the backyard lights on.

And shrieked when they illuminated Horace, standing a foot away from the glass sliding doors, the ram horns still on his head and his eyes seething with rage.

Yeah, okay, I could see why Hank had been growling now.

I froze.

The only thing that came to my mind was my white bubble and I surrounded myself with it right before Horace reached out and slid the door open.

You'd think a girl would've checked the locks to all of her doors when a murderer was on the loose, wouldn't you?

Deciding to take the offensive, I stepped out onto the porch, forcing Horace to take a step back in surprise. I'd seen too many horror movies where the girl gets cornered in her house and flees upstairs. At least this way, I'd be out in the open and my neighbors would hear me scream.

I circled around Horace forcing him to follow me a little further out into the yard, while Hank paced beside me. I really hated that Hank was with me. I didn't care if I got hurt, but I'd lose it if Hank got hurt.

"Horace, lovely to see you again. May I ask why you're hanging out in my backyard?" I asked, easily, keeping my eyes trained on his as I worked to keep the protective bubble intact.

"You left quite suddenly the other night," Horace said slowly, his voice sounding different, more guttural almost, as if he'd smoked six packs of cigarettes and then screamed at a football game all day. I tilted my head and looked at him oddly. Curious now, I reached out and brushed against his mind.

Whoops, probably shouldn't do that. I winced as what sounded like the screams of a thousand people filled my ears and flashes of serpents and flames filled my thoughts. I couldn't decide if this was better or worse than the emptiness that had greeted me the last time I took a little dip into Horace's thoughts.

"Yes, well, things went a little downhill during your 'draw down the moon' ceremony thing, if you'll remember," I said, keeping my distance from Horace but not really sure what to do.

"I'd argue that, and say things actually went exactly the way they were supposed to have gone," Horace said softly.

Frustrated, I shrugged.

"What's your point, Horace? Why are you here creeping in my backyard? You could've called, you know. Super rude," I said.

So about that whole self-preservation thing...

"I like that you have some spunk to you. Your powers benefit from it. It's just too bad I'll need to take them from you."

I held up my hands in front of me to pause him as I

circled, not sure what I was going to do about this little tidbit of information.

"Why do you keep trying to take my power from me? You're clearly so much stronger than I am. What do you need with mine?" Flatter the crazy man. At least I was trying to be smart here.

"Because you're the easiest mark," Horace shook his head at me and sighed, putting his hands on his loincloth. I couldn't help but look down, and yup, Horace seemed to be really excited about stealing my power. The thought grossed me out even more and I gagged a little in my mouth.

"I resent the implication that I'm an easy mark," I argued, continuing to move, forcing Horace away from the house in order to follow me.

"The white witch has a solid wall of protection. I really wanted the Voodoo priestess's power, but it's going to take me a while to get hers. She's a crafty one though. I'll enjoy taking her down," Horace mused.

"Oh, so you're picking on the weak one of the bunch then? Is that it? Then you'll grow stronger with each person you steal power from?"

"Pretty much," Horace said, "It's just like with all my followers. Stupid minions really. It wasn't hard to put a little spell on them to come follow my ways. I've been draining their life energy all year. Last night was supposed to be the moment that I would take all of it."

My mouth dropped open.

"You were going to murder them all?"

"They would have simply vanished. Nobody would've been the wiser," Horace shrugged, no big deal, right?

"Um, their families probably would've noticed," I pointed out, stepping further away from him.

"I tried to pick people that were outliers or who didn't have much family. Either way, what do I care? I was going to be the most powerful one of all. But you ruined that, didn't you Althea? You and your little troop of magickal friends," Horace spit before smiling maniacally at me as he raised his arms over his head, his horns thrown backwards.

Hank darted forward, a savage growl ripping from his furry body, as he sank his teeth into Horace's ankle. I saw Horace's eyes fly open in pain and surprise.

"Hank, come!" I screeched and surprisingly, Hank listened. He darted back to my side as I reached into my bra and threw the pouch I had tucked there for safekeeping. I had no idea what I was doing, but I was out of ideas and Miss Elva's pouches had worked in the past.

A flash of heat, so powerful that it caused Hank and me to stumble backwards, raced into our faces. I scooped Hank into my arms and ran for the beach, terrified we were about to be burned alive.

Knowing I would have to look, I turned to see what had happened, Hank's fuzzy body warm against my chest.

A ring of fire, perfectly formed, surrounded Horace as he beat against an invisible wall.

"What the…" I swore, turning fully and stepping closer so I could see what was happening.

It was like Horace had been enclosed in a cylinder of fire. He beat his fists against the invisible wall, but nothing would shake them. As the flames licked higher into the sky, Horace raised his arms to the sky and screamed.

And in a flash of light – he was gone.

Like, *gone*, gone. Not a dead body on my lawn with a raging fire around him. Just…gone.

The fire disappeared in an instant, and I ran over to look at my battered grass. A small thin circle was all that remained to remind me of what had happened. I blew out a breath, sweat trickling down my face, and pressed my lips into Hank's furry head. Relief coursed through me as I began to shake, delayed shock setting in.

"What the hell?"

I looked up to see Cash's angry face standing in the door to my house. It was the last thing I saw before I went down.

Chapter Thirty-Seven

A WET TONGUE against my face brought me out of it and I looked up at the sky to see Cash's head hovering worriedly over me while Hank licked my face.

"Hank, stop," I protested.

For the second time that night, Cash put his arms beneath my body and lifted me from the ground. It was enough to almost make me faint again.

I looked up at Cash to see his lips pressed together in a tight line. I didn't have to be a mind reader to know he was pissed.

Cash walked inside the door, turning to pull it closed and locking it, and then proceeded to drop me unceremoniously on the couch.

"Hey," I protested, pushing myself up on the cushions. Wasn't I the victim here?

I watched as Cash began to pace the room, his arms swinging in anger.

"Of all the…" he began, and then stopped himself, blowing out a breath.

Hank hopped up on the couch and shoved his nose in my face before moving in next to me to watch the show. His furry body was a comfort to me and I reached out to stroke his back, incredibly grateful he hadn't been hurt by Horace.

"You did a good job, buddy," I whispered to Hank, and he turned and licked my hand, his sandpaper tongue tickling my palm.

"What?" Cash asked, so caught up in his anger that he hadn't heard me.

"Um, nothing. Just telling Hank he was a good boy."

I waited for Cash to speak. I may be stupid sometimes, but I'm not stupid enough to pull the pin on a grenade. And Cash was one big grenade of emotions about to go off over there.

"I come over here to see some madman in horns being eaten by fire, is that correct?" Cash's words came out clipped.

I considered them carefully and then nodded, still not willing to speak.

"Would you care to enlighten me?"

I thought about what Miss Elva had said about not hiding things from the people you love. I didn't know if I loved Cash or not, but I did know there was a lot of potential there. Which meant I couldn't start our relationship based on lies. Gently, I reached out a hand and patted the sofa cushion next to me.

"Why don't you come sit down?"

Cash blew out a breath and ran his hand through his closely cropped hair, causing little pieces to stick up haphazardly.

"Got any beer?"

That sounded excellent right now.

"Yes, and could you get me a glass of wine too?" What? I could play the victim if I wanted.

When Cash finally settled in next to me and I had a cool glass of white wine to soothe my throat, I began to tell him about Horace.

"Wait, he summoned an evil spirit?" Cash's beer was disappearing at an alarming rate as he took in my story.

"So it seems. Now, listen, you have to know this is not what Pagans are or do. He was just a fanatic," I explained, sipping my wine. I didn't want him to hear Luna talk about doing something Pagan-related in the future and have him fly off the deep end.

"Between Horace and the murderer, I've seen more magickal things in 12 hours of being back in Tequila Key than I have in my whole life," Cash said carefully, leveling his eyes at me.

"That you know of," I corrected him, enjoying the cool brush of wine that soothed my throat.

"What do you mean, that I know of?"

"Well, if you aren't in tune with or expecting to see magick, you oftentimes *won't* see the magick," I shrugged.

Cash blew out a breath as he contemplated my words.

"So what happened to that guy?"

"I don't know. That was Miss Elva's magick. I should probably call her," I said, realizing I might need to notify her in case Horace came back.

Cash reached into his pocket and handed me my phone.

"Hey, how'd you get this?"

"You dropped it on the beach."

"My hero," I sang out, delighted that he'd found it. What? Nobody wants to pay those stupid deductibles on the insurance for replacing a lost phone. Plus having to restore all those numbers? I shuddered at the thought.

"Miss Elva," I said, when she answered the call. I could hear Jimmy Buffett in the background and voices laughing.

"You okay, girl?"

"Horace was just here. I used your pouch on him," I said briefly and I heard her quick intake of breath.

"What happened?"

"A cylinder of fire and then he disappeared," I said.

Miss Elva was silent for a moment and I waited.

"Then that was the right one to give you. That's the devil's work, right there. The pouch was meant to match his power so whatever he had going on was reflected at him tenfold."

Huh. Well, wasn't that interesting.

"You are a wealth of surprises, Miss Elva," I finally conceded, too tired to think anymore.

"Child, just be glad you had it. Messing with the underworld is nasty business."

"Is he gone now?"

"Oh, Horace won't be coming back. I suspect the Goddesses are going to take good care of him," Miss Elva chuckled and I felt reassured by her laughter.

"Thanks, Miss Elva."

"You go on and have a good night. Squeeze that hunk of a man and give him a little time to process all this. He'll come around."

I hung up and eyed Cash as I waited for him to say something.

"Ring of fire."

"What's that?" I asked, tilting my head in confusion at him.

"You know, Johnny Cash. Ring of Fire. I fell into a burning ring of fire…" Cash sang creakily and I gaped at him like he'd lost his mind. Cash sighed and rubbed his hands over his face. "I'm tired. But I'm taking the whole ring of fire thing and the correlation with me being named after Johnny Cash as signs from the universe that I'm in the right place. And that's all I can process for the night."

A sign from the universe? Was this really my levelheaded investor boyfriend? I gasped as he stood up and, yes ladies, threw me over his shoulder, taking the stairs two at a time to the bedroom.

Okay, so maybe he wasn't so levelheaded after all.

But it looked like I was about to step into my own ring of fire.

Epilogue

ON THE OTHER side of the Keys, Horace shivered by the side of the road, holding a hand over his privates. He'd woken up naked, scratches covering his long body. He trembled as a flash of headlights crossed his vision and he stood on shaky feet, holding his thumb out.

The car blasted past him, horn blaring, as a soda can flew from the window and landed at his feet, splashing brown liquid across Horace's body.

"Those imbeciles! If only they knew who I was!" Horace seethed, pacing by the side of the road, furious that he had been left alone.

"Where are you, oh mighty one? Why have you forsaken me?" Horace screamed to the sky. He'd been promised a rich life, after all.

A flash of blue light shone from behind him and Horace stiffened, before turning slowly.

A woman, naked but for acres of hair that wound around her, smiled beautifully at him from within her blue glow. She was beautiful in a way not known to man, almost impossible to look directly at.

"Goddess Diana," Horace said, immediately dropping to his knees.

"You've been a naughty boy, Horace," Diana spoke, her voice both wondrous and awful at the same time.

"I know, I'm sorry," Horace whispered.

"Oh, it's far too late for apologies. You've caused some major disturbances in the spiritual world. And opening a portal? Tsk, tsk," Diana clucked as she floated above him.

"I'll close it, I promise. I was wrong," Horace cowered beneath her.

"Oh, you'll close it. When we send you right through it," Diana said, raising her arms.

"No! I don't want to go there," Horace screamed as Diana poured her light into him and he disappeared from the side of the road.

Diana floated for a moment, her eyes trained on the spot where Horace had just been. Sighing, she dusted off her hands and winked out of sight.

Book 2.5 (Novella) in the Althea Rose Mystery Series. Available now!!!

Have you read books from my other series? Join our little community by signing up for updates on island-living, giveaways, and new releases.
http://eepurl.com/1LAiz.

Excerpt from Tequila Will Kill Ya

A Luna & Miss Elva Novella

Book 2.5

"Of course she goes away for Halloween of all things," Luna muttered, thinking about her business partner and best friend, Althea Rose. Luna and Althea co-owned the Luna Rose Potion & Tarot Shop in downtown Tequila Key and Luna was more than a little annoyed with Althea.

"Not like it's one of our busiest times of the year or anything," Luna grumbled as she unpacked a new shipment of crystals. Luna had been surprised when Althea had agreed to go with her boyfriend Cash to Miami for one of his nightclub's Halloween bashes. Psychics were typically in high demand over this holiday and Althea would have made bank on her readings.

Luna supposed that she couldn't necessarily blame Althea. Even if she was a little miffed at her, Luna knew that Althea needed to spend some time in Cash's world too. It would be good for them.

"And because of that, I'm going to close the shop this weekend," Luna announced out loud, smiling down at her pretty display of crystals. It was a bold move for Luna, but business had been good this year and with the launch of her new online ordering system, she'd more than tripled her income. A weekend off was just what she needed. For the first time in years, she'd be really able to celebrate her favorite holiday.

Luna stepped to a low table of reclaimed wood and wiped a smudge from the corner. She loved her shop, the beautiful lines of the whitewashed wood, her pretty displays of candles, and bottles of elixirs with hand crafted white and gold labels. It hit just the right mix of magick and elegance.

Of course, she'd chosen white as her main color, as the color resonated strongly with Luna.

Being a white witch would do that to a person.

And Luna's new Wiccan group had invited her to a very special and extremely exclusive celebration of All Hallows' Eve. When Luna had calculated the lost revenue against the opportunity to take a break from the store and be with witches like her – well, the witches had won.

It would be fun to branch out with a new group.

Available from Amazon

Afterword

Thank you for spending time with my book, I hope you enjoyed the story.

Please consider leaving a review! Your review helps others to take a chance on my stories. I really appreciate your help!

Sign up for information on new releases, free books, and fun giveaways at my website www.triciaomalley.com.

Ms. Bitch

FINDING HAPPINESS IS THE BEST REVENGE

New from Tricia O'Malley
Read Today

From the outside, it seems thirty-six-year-old Tess Campbell has it all. A happy marriage, a successful career as a novelist, and an exciting cross-country move ahead. Tess has always played by the rules and it seems like life is good.

Except it's not. Life is a bitch. And suddenly so is Tess.

"Ms. Bitch is sunshine in a book! An uplifting story of fighting your way through heartbreak and making your own version of happily-ever-after."
~Ann Charles, USA Today Bestselling Author of the Deadwood Mystery Series

"Authentic and relatable, Ms. Bitch packs an emotional punch. By the end, I was crying happy tears and ready to pack my bags in search of my best life."
-Annabel Chase, author of the Starry Hollow Witches series

"It's easy to be brave when you have a lot of support in your life, but it takes a special kind of courage to forge a new path when you're alone. Tess is the heroine I hope I'll be if my life ever crumbles down around me. Ms. Bitch is a journey of determination, a study in self-love, and a hope for second chances. I could not put it down!"
-Renee George, USA Today Bestselling Author of the Nora Black Midlife Psychic Mysteries

"I don't know where to start listing all the reasons why you should read this book. It's empowering. It's fierce.

It's about loving yourself enough to build the life you want. It was honest, and raw, and real and I just...loved it so much!"

– Sara Wylde, author of Fat

The Althea Rose Series

ALSO BY TRICIA O'MALLEY

One Tequila

Tequila for Two

Tequila Will Kill Ya (Novella)

Three Tequilas

Tequila Shots & Valentine Knots (Novella)

Tequila Four

A Fifth of Tequila

A Sixer of Tequila

Seven Deadly Tequilas

Available in audio, e-book & paperback!

Available from Amazon

"Not my usual genre but couldn't resist the Florida Keys setting. I was hooked from the first page. A fun read with just the right amount of crazy! Will definitely follow this series."- Amazon Review

The Mystic Cove Series

ALSO BY TRICIA O'MALLEY

Wild Irish Roots (Novella, Prequel)

Wild Irish Heart

Wild Irish Eyes

Wild Irish Soul

Wild Irish Rebel

Wild Irish Roots: Margaret & Sean

Wild Irish Witch

Wild Irish Grace

Wild Irish Dreamer

Wild Irish Sage

Available in audio, e-book & paperback!

Available from Amazon

"I have read thousands of books and a fair percentage have been romances. Until I read Wild Irish Heart, I never had a book actually make me believe in love."- Amazon Review

The Isle of Destiny Series

ALSO BY TRICIA O'MALLEY

Stone Song

Sword Song

Spear Song

Sphere Song

Available in audio, e-book & paperback!

Available from Amazon

"Love this series. I will read this multiple times. Keeps you on the edge of your seat. It has action, excitement and romance all in one series."- Amazon Review

The Siren Island Series

ALSO BY TRICIA O'MALLEY

Good Girl

Up to No Good

A Good Chance

Good Moon Rising

Too Good To Be True

Available in audio, e-book & paperback!

Available from Amazon

"Love her books and was excited for a totally new and different one! Once again, she did NOT disappoint! Magical in multiple ways and on multiple levels. Her writing style, while similar to that of Nora Roberts, kicks it up a notch!! I want to visit that island, stay in the B&B and meet the gals who run it! The characters are THAT real!!!" - Amazon Review

Author's Note

Thank you for taking a chance on my books; it means the world to me. Writing novels came by way of a tragedy that turned into something beautiful and larger than itself (see: *The Stolen Dog*). Since that time, I've changed my career, put it all on the line, and followed my heart.

Thank you for taking part in the worlds I have created; I hope you enjoy it.

I would be honored if you left a review online. It helps other readers to take a chance on my work.

As always, you can reach me at info@triciaomalley.com or feel free to visit my website at www.triciaomalley.com.

Author's Acknowledgement

First, and foremost, I'd like to thank my family and friends for their constant support, advice, and ideas. You've all proven to make a difference on my path. And, to my beta readers, I love you for all of your support and fascinating feedback!

And last, but never least, my two constant companions as I struggle through words on my computer each day - Briggs and Blue.

Printed in Great Britain
by Amazon